JEANNE GOOSEN

We're not all like that

Translated from the Afrikaans by
ANDRÉ BRINK

KWELA BOOKS

Any resemblance between

characters and people

living or dead is purely coincidental – JG

Kwela Books,
a division of NB Publishers (Pty) Limited,
40 Heerengracht, Cape Town, South Africa
PO Box 6525, Roggebaai, 8012, South Africa
http://www.kwela.com

Cover design by Michiel Botha, Flame
Cover photo from Gallo Images
Typography by Nazli Jacobs
Set in Utopia
Printed and bound by Paarl Print,
Oosterland Street, Paarl, South Africa

Originally published in Afrikaans by Queillerie in 1990
First English edition published by Queillerie in 1992
Second edition, first impression 2007

ISBN-10: 0-7957-0259-0
ISBN-13: 978-0-7957-0259-4

Continually I try to write it down,

this sense of family life. For it seems to me

that the funny voices we make with our mouths,

or the squiggles that we put on paper,

are only for ourselves to hear, to prove

there's someone there.

BERYL BAINBRIDGE

PART ONE

MY MOM AND AUNT MAVIS pull up beside the chicken run in my dad's Plymouth. They're kicking up such a row laughing and talking that old Mrs Haasbroek's dog opposite starts barking.

'Shoosh!' shouts Aunt Mavis.

They come in through the back door.

'Have you been a good girl?' asks my mom. She takes a parcel from her bag, holds it up against the light and reads: 'Which twin has the Tony?'

Aunt Mavis puts on the kettle for tea. 'Gee, Doris,' she says, 'you promise you going to make a good job on my perm, hey?'

'Don't fear when Doris is near,' laughs my mom. 'Gertie,' she tells me, 'go and get us some small plates.' She takes three doughnuts from a paper bag.

Aunt Mavis sets out the cups and my mom puts a doughnut on each plate. We sit down at the kitchen table.

'Nothing to beat the Homepride's doughnuts,' says Aunt Mavis through a full mouth.

'Is my girlie enjoying it?' asks my mom, leaning over to kiss me.

Aunt Mavis lightly taps my head with her teaspoon. 'Little Blue-eyes!'

I laugh. My mom and Aunt Mavis can be so funny.

'Gertie,' says my mom, 'go get us the tall mirror from our bedroom, then you can sit there on the floor with your puzzle. We're going to perm Aunt Mavis's hair.' She touches her own hair, her eyes huge. 'Old Tank won't know his girl when he sees her tonight. He'll be seasick from all the waves.'

My mom and Aunt Mavis work evenings and one Saturday afternoon a month at the matinées in the Victoria bioscope in Parow. They're usherettes.

Aunt Mavis is my mom's best friend. They wear black skirts and white blouses when they usher. They also wear flat round hats on the back of their heads, held in place with hairpins. They're not really hats. It's more like the small round baking pans in which my mom makes cake when my grandpa comes to visit. Only deeper.

Aunt Mavis is fat and jolly. When she lights a Cavalla she blows the smoke out through her nose. She drops in almost every morning. Sometimes she and my mom sit on the floor in the sitting room listening to records on our Pilot. What they like is musicals like *Showboat* and *Naughty Marietta*.

My mom has every record ever made by Jeanette MacDonald and Nelson Eddy. Every time she plays 'Maytime' she and Aunt Mavis join in when Jeanette MacDonald comes to the bit about 'Sweetheart, sweetheart'. Then their eyes get full of tears.

'Nothing like true love,' Aunt Mavis says every time.

My mom doesn't say anything, she just sits staring in front of her. My mom also has a record of Richard Tauber singing. The song is called 'For you alone'. When my mom is really feeling sad, that's the record she plays. I once heard her telling Aunt Mavis that my dad bought her the record when they were still engaged.

'Piet was such a romantic, you know, Mavis. You'd never think it was the same man you see there today.' She wipes the tears from her eyes and blows her nose.

'Ag shame, Doris man,' says Aunt Mavis. 'Who knows, perhaps it'll all come back once he's over it all. You never know.'

'Whenever he came over he always brought something. Always a surprise. Like chocolates, Black Magic, or sometimes flowers, once even a bowl with goldfish in it.' My mom gets up, takes two glasses from the shelf and says to Aunt Mavis, 'Ag man, let's have a drink.'

At other times my mom and Aunt Mavis spend their time knitting at the kitchen table. Aunt Mavis is forever knitting pullovers for Uncle Tank, complaining about his long arms. It's cables they knit, with three needles. They count the stitches in English, marking off the rows on the *Woman's Weekly* patterns in pencil. Sometimes my mom pours them rum from the bottle my dad uses for his chest before he goes to bed at night.

Uncle Tank is Aunt Mavis's boyfriend. I think he's younger than her, at least that's what I heard my mom tell my dad. He has a big belly, and a moustache, and he parts his hair in the middle. He and Aunt Mavis always mix their English and Afrikaans. They're renting two rooms from Mrs Bonthuys a bit further down, in Watering Street.

Uncle Tank has trouble finding a job and Aunt Mavis says it makes him depressed. He has only one foot and he hobbles along. My mom says it's the enemy who shot off his left foot in the war. That was up North. He gets a war pension, but Aunt Mavis says it isn't enough for them to live on.

Almost every day Uncle Tank is out looking for a job. Sometimes when Isaac Levitt needs a driver up at the chicken feed factory he sends a message to Uncle Tank. Then he drives the lorry for a couple of days, just as long as they need him, dropping off chicken feed at the shops.

Some mornings on his way back from looking for work Uncle Tank turns up at our place with a bottle of Old Brown sherry from which he pours for himself and Aunt Mavis and my mom at the kitchen table.

Then Uncle Tank tells them how very nearly he got the job. 'You might say I already had it in my hands, but at the last moment they found out about my foot and then it was tickets.'

He takes another mouthful of sherry and gets up, leaning forward a bit. 'It's bad luck,' he says. He blows his nose, fills up his glass again, and sits down.

'Cruel world,' says Aunt Mavis, lighting a Cavalla and blowing out the smoke through her nose.

'You know, Doris,' says Uncle Tank, 'here I'm standing before you, a man with two hands, willing and able, but do you think there's anyone in this life prepared to listen to another man's story? Not a damn. It's not enough for them to see you begging. Oh no, they've got to squash you. And then we've got this government too,' adds Uncle Tank. 'But you just listen to me, mark my words, I'm giving them another two years and no more. That's all.' He points a finger at my mom. 'That's not the way to treat people, not even if they're kaffirs. What a life for the poor bastards!' Uncle Tank gets up again, but Aunt Mavis pushes him back into the chair.

'Don't get so upset, Tank. Things will work out eventually, man.'

My dad doesn't like Uncle Tank and Aunt Mavis. I heard him telling my mom that they're living together like man and wife. Mavis is bad enough, says my dad, but that Tank, he's a bladdie communist.

My mom says it's the war that made Uncle Tank the way he is, but once you get to know him, he isn't such a bad old stick, she's got nothing against him. Actually she rather likes him.

I must say, I'm also fond of Uncle Tank and it's quite true, my dad doesn't know him properly. When he comes to visit he always pinches my nose and says, 'Hello, Monkeyface! Give us a smile.' Sometimes he gives me money to buy cigarette sweets. Then I sit on the kitchen floor and every time my mom and them light their Cavallas I put a cigarette sweet in my mouth and start sucking, holding my elbow in my other hand.

They say that once, just after the war, Uncle Tank spent two months in jail. He and another man caught birds in a trap, and then dyed them and sold them, telling people they were Australian sparrows.

When it started raining the dye came off and that's how Uncle Tank and the other man got caught. Actually the dye cost them just as much as they got for the birds, and if you add up all the trouble as well, he's not so sure it was a good idea, says Uncle Tank.

'It was just bad luck on my side,' he says. 'That's all. Bad luck.'

Aunt Mavis says Uncle Tank can get very down in the dumps. 'This thing with his foot gets him down, Doris,' says Aunt Mavis. 'And you know what men are like, never show their feelings. I know Tank can get on one's nerves at times, but he's a good sort, really.'

Uncle Tank is good at playing the guitar and singing. He can sing Italian opera and croon like Bing Crosby. And he can also imitate Al Jolson. When he sings 'There was blood on the saddle' or when he yodels you'd think he was a real cowboy. Like Gene Autrey.

He and Aunt Mavis and my mom are sitting here at the kitchen table having a drink, and soon Aunt Mavis will be saying, 'Tank, give us a song, chum. Come on, please man.'

Then Uncle Tank starts singing and playing. He sings 'Mammy', his eyes filling with tears. Afterwards he sings 'You are my sunshine, my only sunshine', just the way Bing Crosby sings it. And then he sings Italian. He sings 'Back to Sorrento', 'O sole mio' and 'Santa Lucia'. Uncle Tank has to sing 'Santa Lucia' over and over. It's Aunt Mavis's favourite.

When he's finished singing he fills up his glass again and sits down. Then he wipes his face with his handkerchief.

My mom says, 'Tank, you've got a great talent. You're a truly gifted man.'

Uncle Tank says, 'Doris, I could've gone professional, you know. But what do you know, then the war broke out and from then on it was just bad luck for this boy. Everybody says I ought to be on the stage, but Doris, be honest, who wants to see a performer with one foot missing? Tell me. Come on. Tell me . . .!'

'Ag never mind, Tankie,' says Aunt Mavis, touching his shoulder. 'One day your ship will come. Just wait and see.'

Aunt Mavis sits down on Uncle Tank's lap, her arms round his neck. 'Hey, cheer up, man, come on! Give your Mavis a kiss!' She presses her nose into Uncle Tank's neck and says, 'Kissy, kissy, kissy!' until he starts laughing again.

He looks at my mom. 'Doris, look at this.' Then he sort of chuckles and says, 'Woman . . .!'

Shortly before lunch Uncle Tank and Aunt Mavis get up to go. Uncle Tank takes his guitar, slides his arm through Aunt Mavis's, and off they go.

'Cheerio, Monkeyface!' he says to me. 'Stay as sweet as you are.'

My mom became an usherette after my dad had the accident on the trains. It happened near De Aar and my dad says it was all the shunter's fault because he'd been sleeping on the job. My dad was driving the engine. Through the accident he got gas in his lungs and nearly died. The doctors couldn't do anything for my dad. They gave him six months, so the Railways boarded him.

When my mom started working her youngest sister, Aunt Mietjie, moved in with us so she could look after me and my dad in the evenings when my mom had to catch the train in to Cape Town. She got a job at the Roxy T-room where she worked night shift. My mom had always been fond of bioscope and when my dad fell ill it was the first place she went to look for work.

My Aunt Mietjie says she doesn't know what's going to become of my mom and this thing she has about bioscopes. 'It's because your grandpa used to be so strict with us. We weren't allowed to do anything because it was all sinful, and now you're stuck with a mother who can't stay out of the bioscope.

'I don't know where it's going to end,' says my Aunt Mietjie, spreading the butter on the slice of bread, over and over. 'But it's all your grandpa's fault, is what I say. One's got to make sure your kids get used to everything while they're still small. Which is why I always say prove all things, hold fast that which is good.'

Aunt Mietjie is the head girl in a cigarette factory in Koeberg, but she doesn't smoke. My mom says she got promoted very soon because she's so quick with her hands.

Aunt Mietjie has a boyfriend who comes over every evening. They spend the whole evening in the sitting room, talking quietly so as not to disturb my dad. Late at night, before he leaves, his name is Uncle Koos, she makes tea and brings me a cup to my room too. Then she gives me pink sweets from a canned fruit bottle she keeps up in her wardrobe. Every evening before she goes to bed she tucks me in and says, 'Poor child . . .'

One night my mom doesn't come home at the usual time. Aunt Mietjie puts on all the lights in the house and wakes me up. Then we go to sit on the stoep waiting for my mom. Every now and then my dad calls Aunt Mietjie from the bedroom. 'Shit, Mietjie,' he says at last, 'it's past two. Where's Doris? Man, shouldn't we call the police?'

'Let's wait another fifteen minutes, Piet,' says Aunt Mietjie and she shouts at me to go out in the street to see if she isn't coming yet. 'Look hard, Gertie, you've got better eyes than me.'

I stay in the street for a long time and sometimes it seems as if someone is coming, so I keep waiting, but in the end it's nothing. I'm still standing there staring into the dark when I notice someone moving way down in the street near the Spiro Café, but it doesn't look like my mom's way of walking. The person down there is moving like an old woman.

Only when the person stops right in front of our gate I realise it's my mom after all.

'Ma-a-a!' I cry, scared by her face and the way she looks.

My Aunt Mietjie also comes running to the gate.

My mom presses me against her.

'My God, Doris!' says my Aunt Mietjie.

'Jeez, Mietjie,' says my mom, 'I'm pooped, man. Tonight I really hit rock bottom.'

'You come in first, Doris,' says my Aunt Mietjie, taking my mom by the arm. 'Piet's beside himself with worrying. Come on in, I'll put the kettle on for some tea.'

As my mom comes in through the front door my dad shouts from the bedroom, 'Doris, is this the time for a decent woman to come home . . .?'

My mom goes to him, walking very fast and straight. I can see she's in a rage.

'Shut up, you!' she yells at him. 'Will you give me a break? Do you mind? Can't you see what I look like?'

My mom tears off her overcoat, throws it over the chair and takes off her beret.

'But where . . .' my dad tries to ask.

'I told you to shut up! And if you don't I'll just take my things and go, I swear to God!' She goes through to the kitchen, pulls out a chair and sits down at the table.

I can see the tears running down her face, her shoulders shaking, but she makes no sound.

My Aunt Mietjie sits down opposite her with the tea and the cups. 'Doris?'

'It's okay, Mietjie, it's all okay,' my mom says. 'I got locked up in that bladdie Roxy.'

'My God, Doris!' my aunt says again.

'Ja. You see, after the show I went to the Ladies to powder my nose and so on, you know. But when I came out everybody had left and the doors were locked. Jeez, I had a go at those doors, pulling and rattling and shouting, but no luck. Not a soul in sight, man.

'Mietjie, do you have any idea of what goes through one's mind in a dead and empty bioscope like that? Can you imagine it? No, you can't, but you ask me. Let me tell you. It's worse than hell.'

Aunt Mietjie starts pouring the tea.

'So what could I do? I just sat down in one of the back seats. Tried to think. By then I was really scared. And you know, it was a Frankenstein movie they showed tonight. My hair was up on end. It felt like something I couldn't see was creeping up behind me. Something, I could hear it breathing. I'm not lying to you. And upstairs in the operator's cubicle I could hear someone walking. Slowly, like a murderer. I don't know how long I sat there. All I can tell you is that I prayed like I never prayed in my life before. Even promised the Lord I'd give up bioscope. And even the Cavallas.'

'Have some tea, Doris,' says Aunt Mietjie, pushing the cup towards my mom. 'Drink. It'll do you good.'

'Like I said, I don't know how long I sat there, but all of a sudden something struck me. The phone! If one's as scared as that you don't think straight, man. I tell you, I just got up and ran to the manager's office and thank the Lord he hadn't locked it. I got hold of the phone book, but I was trembling so much it took a long time before I found the number of the police. They said they'd send old Byrd to come and unlock the place for me.

'And so there I stood waiting at the door for old Byrd, and it felt like hours I stood there. I read all the posters in the foyer and I tell you, man, if I close my eyes I can still see Rita Hayworth in her bubble bath.

'Then at long last Byrd turned up with his bunch of keys, and did he give me a talking to! Laid into me, left, right and centre, and what could I do, I mean I needed his help. And was I crying!

'So I went to the station, but by that time the last train had gone, of course. All on my own I started walking and Mietjie, you should have seen the looks the sailors gave me. Know what I mean?'

'You must be flaked, Doris,' says Aunt Mietjie. 'Shame, man.'

'Anyway, to cut a long story short, at the bottom end of the platform I found a man in uniform and I told him my story.

'No, he tells me in a whiny little voice, no I'm sorry, Madam, but you see the last train's gone, so I really don't know . . .

'"I know that, Mister," I tell him, and then, all of a sudden, right there, I got mad. I grabbed him by the collar and I told him, "Look, Mister, I got a sick husband at home, and a child. I don't give a damn how you do it, but you got to think of something. I *must* get home before this night is over."'

'The turd!' says Aunt Mietjie.

'That made him wake up all right. "Well," he said, "all right, Madam, there's a goods-train going that way, but it only leaves in ten minutes."

'"I'll take it," I say. All right then, he says, he'll see what he can do. He'll speak to the driver and ask him to stop at Elsies so I can get off there.

'So there I end up in the goods-train in the guards' van with two guards, and I'd rather not tell you about the way they stared at me. You can think for yourself, hey, a woman on her own, that time of the night, no, the morning.'

My mom starts sobbing again.

'Ag shame, Doris,' says Aunt Mietjie. 'At least you're home now and that's the main thing. Now drink your tea, and tomorrow's another day.'

'And then Piet talks to me like that. He doesn't care about *me*. Oh no! Maybe I'll get punished for saying this, but there are times I hate that man. He has no idea of the price I got to pay for all this. There he's lying ill in his bed, and I've got to look after him, and clean the house, and do the washing and the ironing, and see that Gertie gets brought up in a proper way, and then he puts on that attitude. Heaven knows, Mietjie, what will I have in this world if it wasn't for the bioscope?'

'Bioscope is in your mom's blood,' Aunt Mietjie tells me. 'Shame, she doesn't have much of a life what with your dad and all.

'D'you know your mom was in the papers once? It was with *Gone with the Wind* and Vivien Leigh. The picture was shown here in Cape Town. It began in the Alhambra. Your mom was quite crazy about that film. Night after night, time and time again, she went to see it. That was well before she started ushering. All she could talk about was *Gone with the Wind*. After some time they took it off and it was shown in another bioscope, and each time the film moved on your mom followed. Wherever *Gone with the Wind* went, she went too.

'She went to see it in Woodstock, in Salt River, then in Maitland, Goodwood, later in Parow and even in Bellville. In the end your mom saw it more than thirty times and every single night she came home with her eyes red from crying.

'Actually I think it was in Bellville – I'm not quite sure, but anyway –

the manager came to notice your mom standing right in front of the queue every night. So one evening he spoke to her and she told him how many times she'd seen *Gone with the Wind*.

'And that was when he phoned the newspaper. The *Argus* it was. So they sent a man and he took a snap of your mom in front of the bioscope with the poster of *Gone with the Wind*. And they put that picture with your mom's story in the paper, just like that.

'So what happened was all the Cape Town managers got together and decided that from then on your mom could see *Gone with the Wind* wherever it showed in the city. For free.

'Afterwards your mom said to me, "Mietjie," she said, "I would have gone all the way up to Jo'burg for *Gone with the Wind*. If I could, I mean."'

After a while the six months of my dad's illness is over. Doctor Hoffman says it's a miracle. My dad's been getting better and better all the time, but he's still boarded. He's stranded without a job and things just can't go on like this, he says. Not with him staying at home and my mom out in the bioscope night after night until God knows what hour.

My dad's a Ben Schoeman man. This Ben Schoeman is a big name in the Railways. He's real high up, my dad always says, and he's sure the man can do something for him. When Ben Schoeman says something, people listen. At the time my dad was still a stoker he met Ben Schoeman personally. That was at a meeting and afterwards my dad had a long talk with him.

So now my dad writes this Ben Schoeman a long letter to explain the whole thing and he also sends a certificate from Doctor Hoffman to say that my dad's definitely well enough to do a full day's work.

One day, a long time after my dad has written, a letter arrives in the mail. The letter tells my dad to go to Salt River at such and such a time on such and such a date to see such and such a man. They'll talk to him. When the day comes my dad puts on his best suit and right early in the morning, long before the time they told him to, he's off on the train. He stays away all day and it's late afternoon before he comes home again.

He's got a job all right, he tells my mom at the table. But what a job! All they could do for him, my dad says, was to make him a flag-man at the Tiervlei crossing near the high school.

'It's a disgrace!' says my dad. 'I'm a man with rank! Engine driver. I'm an engine driver! I belong right there on the footplates! So who do they think Piet van Greunen is? Just a nobody? Is that what they expect me to do from now on? Wave a red flag at a crossing? This is the last time I vote for this government!'

My mom talks to him very nicely. 'Ag Piet,' she says, 'try to think about it like this, man: work is something noble. This is the way it goes when they see you're down, but it's not the end of the world. You're still young enough and things will come right again. It's no good just sitting here with nothing to do. So why don't you maar take the job, just for a start? That way you can earn something until you're up and about again – and by that time you can find another job.

'We should be grateful, you know, that you still have two hands to work with. Things could have been worse. And in the end everything will work out all right. You'll see, Piet.'

My dad takes the job, but every evening he complains and then my mom has to plead with him again.

Since that accident at De Aar my dad's changed a lot. He never laughs any more and he almost never talks to us. For days on end he goes around moping. And after the accident he started getting asthma. Mom says it's because of the gas that got into his lungs. Nowadays he's better, only the asthma is still there.

The Railways' sick fund gave him a pump with two tubes, one for each nostril. Whenever he feels an attack coming on he must push the tubes up his nose and start pumping. The pump makes a funny screeching sound. But it helps, says my mom, and that's all that matters.

Many nights I wake up from the screeching of the pump, then I know my dad's having another attack. It's really getting him down and that, says my mom, is why he is the way he is now.

My mom says the accident has given my dad a terrible blow. Engines are my dad's life. That's what made him a man. They kind of made up for his being so short. I mustn't think badly of my dad, my mom says. He's got many good points. He doesn't drink, he brings his money home, and he doesn't beat her, his wife. I'm still a child, my mom says, I'm too young to understand what a thing like that can do to a man. Because, my mom says, my dad's a man who wants to get on in the world. Actually he's a very bright man, but he's never

24

had a chance. When he was only fourteen he was already an orphan, and done out of his inheritance.

'Your dad comes from a very good home. His people were well-to-do. Smart. They even dressed for dinner. There was a time when the whole of Claremont belonged to your dad's grandpa Piet van Greunen. Then that thing happened between his father, your grandpa, and his third wife, who was a Grobbelaar . . .'

I've never found out about this thing that happened and which caused my dad to lose everything and to miss out on the chances he deserved.

All I know is that it isn't nice at all, the way my dad became after the train accident. Ever since then the kids don't want to come and play at our place any more, and that Jacobs lot keep on complaining that my dad gives them dirty looks. For my mom's sake I never say anything, because her life's hard enough as it is. I just have to wait, my mom says, sooner or later my dad will once again be what he used to be and then he'll take us to Campers Paradise in the Plymouth for picnics. Once my dad's got rid of the asthma and gets back on his own train he'll be all right again.

Before the accident we often went to Campers Paradise. My mom says Campers Paradise is a very special place for my dad. That is because one Boxing Day the Minister made the train my dad was on the Mystery Train. In those days, you see, my dad was still a young man and he and my mom had just started to go out. He was still a stoker then. My mom says the Cape Town people always used to meet under the big clock at Cape Town station on Boxing Day with their picnic hampers. Then they could have a free ride to some place to have a picnic. Because nobody knew beforehand where the train would take them they used to call it the Mystery Train. Then the Minister arrived on the platform in his smart suit and took out a letter and read out the names of the engine driver and the stoker whose engine was the shiniest and the best all year, and then they were appointed to take the people to their picnic spot in the Mystery Train. And that one year it was my dad's train that was chosen and they had to take the crowd to Campers Paradise.

It was really my dad's prize, says my mom, because it's the stoker's job to keep the engine clean and running. And if ever there was a tidy man it was my dad, says my mom, so the prize was a great honour for him.

My mom says she was also on that Mystery Train that special Boxing Day and it was a wonderful day. All the way there and back the people sang. Everybody spoke to everybody. They were laughing and dancing in the passages of the train. The whole train was made up with balloons and streamers, there was even a Christmas tree. And my dad was in great shape, he really performed. At Campers Paradise everybody came to congratulate him. And my mom says the engine driver, a Mr Vaughan, thought very highly of my dad. He called my dad Peter.

My mom also says they hung a mistletoe in the engine where my dad and Mr Vaughan were sitting. And when they came to Campers Paradise Mr Vaughan specially fetched her to come and have a look inside the engine so that she could see what kind of a job my dad was working at. My mom says when she climbed up the steps into the engine my dad grabbed her and kissed her, just like that. A whole lot of people were watching.

Gee, she was embarrassed, says my mom, because at that time she'd just started to go out with my dad. My dad burst out laughing and he said, 'But Doris, I've *got* to kiss you, man, you're standing right under the mistletoe!'

My mom also says that all the way to Campers Paradise and back the train kept on whistling. They waved at all the people they passed on the stations, shouting Happy New Year to them.

She can't think of a single other day in her life she's enjoyed so much, my mom says. And there were all sorts of women eyeing my dad that day, but he only looked at her.

Late that night, totally flaked, they got back to Cape Town station, but what a marvellous, marvellous day it'd been, says my mom, staring up at the ceiling with shining eyes.

There's something else too. That Boxing Day they took loads of snaps on the station – of the engine driver and my dad and the Minister and of other people I can't remember now. They also took a snap of my dad with the steam engine. He's standing with one foot on the steps, one hand on his hip, and the other holding the engine door. It's a lovely snapshot and on it I can see that my dad used to be a really handsome man when he still went out with my mom.

My dad had an enlargement made of the snapshot and then he had it framed. It hangs in our passage right opposite the round mirror, so you can see my dad and his engine twice when you come in at the front door.

He really is a clever man, my dad. People used to come all the way from Vasco and Green Arrow so my dad could help them fill in the forms they couldn't understand. Then my dad gave them a hand and explained to them what to do. Some people wanted my dad to help them with business letters, he even had to write it for them. Then my dad wrote those letters in a very learned way and read them back to the people.

He's just as good with English. Almost better, in fact, because my dad's family used to speak English at home. And then he even understands High Dutch well. My dad also has a beautiful handwriting. Everybody used to talk about it, even the principal at Parow Primary. Very fine, almost like a woman's, says my mom.

My dad has never been one to mix with the neighbours. He never greets the Haasbroeks or Maizie Vlooi and her family. Actually he never talks to anybody in the street, except sometimes to old Kok Bok opposite. When he goes out he lifts his head right up in the air, pretending not to see anyone.

'Gee, Piet, man,' my mom says sometimes, 'they're our neighbours after all. You're so stuck-up. What if something happens and we need each other? I mean, it's like the Bible says . . .'

'They're not our class,' my dad answers. 'Birds of a feather, as they say. Anyway, Doris, if you really want me to mix with that lot, you try to bring me one – just one! – who can conduct a proper conversation!'

Then my mom falls silent. She sits at the dining table, smoking, a wrinkle between her two eyes.

'It's my conviction that a person always has to try and improve his station in life,' says my dad. 'So one mixes with those who have something to teach you. That's the only way.'

My dad's been waving his flag for almost a year at the Tiervlei crossing when one night he comes home and tells my mom he's now had enough of it all. He's beginning to lose his self-respect because everybody treats him like dirt. 'You'd swear I was a hotnot, the way the inspector spoke to me today,' says my dad.

'Don't talk like that in front of the child,' says my mom. 'And I don't want you to say kaffir either. It's "native". Kaffir and hotnot are words full of hate. Rather say "native" and "coloured".'

My dad puts in for leave, because now he's got to think up something, he says. Piet van Greunen cannot let people mess him around.

The next day my dad goes off to Doctor Hoffmann for a proper examination. And he comes home with a certificate that says he has now recovered completely. He's as healthy as he used to be before the accident, and Doctor Hoffmann recommends that the Van Greunen case be looked at again, very thoroughly. They must give him a proper job.

That evening my dad sits down at the dining table to write another letter. In the middle of the night, when I get up for a drink of water, I find my dad still sitting there, writing. So it must be a very long letter indeed.

When I get up in the morning my dad has already been to the post office to post the letter.

After a few days my dad starts waiting outside to meet the mailman, and one morning a letter comes. He must present himself, once again, in Salt River, the letter says. Such and such a day, such and such a time.

So he goes in to town, in a new suit, new maroon tie and maroon waistcoat and everything, and his hair cut short.

In Salt River they make him do tests all day long. He has to fill in a whole heap of forms, and do arithmetic, and fit things together the way a child builds a jigsaw puzzle, my dad says, but in the end it's no good, because they refuse to put him back on the trains again. Still, in a way my dad doesn't feel quite so bad, because it hasn't been altogether useless. They're giving him another job, a much better one than flagman, with a much bigger salary *and* with a rank: stock verifier. What's more, he'll now have a chance to work himself up.

Actually it's quite an important job, my dad says at the dining table. He'll be sort of his own boss at the Woodstock Railway Supplies where they're going to station him. In that job he'll be responsible for every nail and screw and bolt and hammer and pliers and whatever they keep in that store. He'll even have an office, because for everything that goes out or comes in there's dispatch and delivery forms, receipts and invoices.

My dad is good at his work. That's what many people he meets there say when they come to our house. A man who lives close by – everybody calls him old Cottage Pie – tells my mom that after my dad had been at Supplies for barely two months there was no-one who could teach him anything. My dad, he says, just takes one look at a load of screws or bolts to tell exactly how many there are, and he's never more than one or two out.

His stock book is always one hundred per cent correct, the figures written in neat columns so that anyone can make out what it says. No-one can ever catch him out with a wrong sum.

'And tidy, that Piet of yours, Doris,' says old Cottage Pie, 'everything in its place. You've hardly said a word before Piet puts his hand right on it. You can eat off the floor of that place. He's really a nifty one.'

After a few months my dad writes his exam. He passes well and gets upgraded. They also give him a raise and now our house is really beginning to look up inside.

We get a new lounge suite in white wood. The coffee table is shaped like a kidney. Under the coffee table, which is in the middle of the floor, are three more tables, only smaller. Also like kidneys, each fitting into the others. One chair has a yellow cushion, the second a red one, the third a green one, and the settee is grey. In front of the window new curtains are hung – also one yellow, and the other three red, green and grey to match the chairs and the settee.

My dad does the kitchen up too, and cupboards are built in and for her birthday my mom gets a Hoover washing machine.

Some evenings my Aunt Mietjie comes to sleep at our house, and then my mom and dad go out for the evening. My mom buys herself a beautiful overcoat, a purple one cut wide at the back, with pleats.

Although things are getting better they're still not right. My dad isn't friendly any more and the asthma doesn't go away. What is more, he's getting even more quiet and glum than before. He hardly ever speaks to me any more, just scowls at me, saying things like, 'Sit like a girl!' or, 'Go and wash your face!'

One day my mom stays out all morning. By lunchtime she comes home, but she's very quiet.

She seems to be thinking all the time. I try to talk to her, but she doesn't hear me, or otherwise she just asks, 'What was that you said, Gertie?'

My mom puts on the food, my dad comes home from work and we sit down for lunch, but my mom stays quiet. Halfway through the meal she suddenly says, 'Look, Piet, I don't care what you say, but from Saturday night I'm going ushering again.'

My mom says it in such a way that I know she's made up her mind. She is going to usher, and nothing and no-one will stop her.

My dad looks up; he has stopped chewing.

'I'm not going to stay here at home,' says my mom. 'Life is passing me by and what am I getting out of it?'

My dad doesn't answer. Leaving his plate of food just like that, he gets up, walks out the back door and goes to water the garden.

My mom takes me by the chin and turns my face to her. 'And you, my little Gertie?' she asks. 'You're not going to begrudge me a bit of fun in life, are you?'

I shake my head to and fro, and smile. 'Aunt Mietjie says the bioscope is in your blood.'

My mom bursts out laughing, gets up, takes money from the drawer in the dresser and gives it to me. Then she kisses me, and says, 'A real little shrewdie you are. Bladdie little shrewdie.'

So that's when my mom started ushering in Parow. At the Victoria bioscope, two blocks from our house. And that's where she met Aunt Mavis and where our lives began to change.

'You know, Piet,' I hear my mom telling my dad at the table one day, 'Mavis has had a bad time too. She was engaged to this soldier, you see. They were all set to get married when they sent him off to Italy. And he'd just got there when he was killed.

'By the time Mavis got the news, she was already knocked up. And you know how it is with people, hey. Her mother, her father, her whole family, all her friends, everybody just turned their backs on her. Rejected her. And then she also lost her job at the CTC Bazaar in Plein Street. In the end she landed in the Magdalena Home with almost sweet blow-all to her name.

'Then the baby was born, it was a girl, but from the beginning you could tell there was something wrong. The child wasn't all there, you know. Kind of different from other kids.

'Mavis was already working again when one day she took the child in to the doctor. It was for something else altogether. The croup, I think. Anyway, that's when the doctor told her that Caroline, that was the baby's name, that she was a mongol. He wanted Mavis to send the child to the Alexandra.

'Mavis was terribly upset. Over her dead body, she said. Caroline was all she had. Life had turned its back on her and the child was all she had left and the only one who loved her.

'Hell, Piet, it's so damn sad, Mavis showed me the snapshots.

'Mavis worked her hands to the bone for that child, but in the end she couldn't take it any more. It all just got too much for her. From all the worrying she couldn't do her job properly any more either, so when the till in the haberdashery where she worked was short again, the manager sacked her.

'And in the end poor little Caroline was sent to the Alexandra. It's like Mavis still cannot get over it, you know, as if she cannot forgive herself. The child is almost ten now, but every Sunday Mavis still catches the train to the Alexandra to visit her.

'Ag, poor Mavis,' sighs my mom. She gets up and turns on the kettle for coffee.

My dad is still eating. He's carved all the meat from the bone without saying a word, but all the while one could see he was listening.

'Now Tank is there, thank heavens,' my mom goes on. 'But you know, Piet, I understand and yet I don't understand either. This thing with Tank. Mavis is very fond of Tank. In her way. Actually, I don't think she can cross a street without Tank, but still she doesn't want to think of marrying him.

'And Tank's the same. He worships the ground Mavis walks on and if she were to tell him, "Tank, go fetch me the moon," I'm sure he'll get up straight away and say, "Okay, Mavis, I'll be right back."

'He's given up asking her, Tank has, because Mavis keeps on saying no. So as I said, I understand and yet I don't understand either. Why d'you think it's like that, Piet?'

My dad still doesn't answer.

My mom gets up to pour the coffee into the cups. She sits down again and lights a Cavalla. 'Oh well,' she sighs, 'other people's doings are a mystery.'

My dad puts down the chop bone and pushes his plate away. He wipes his mouth with the back of his hand, pulls his coffee closer, and says, 'Listen, Doris, I think it's a good thing that you brought this up and asked me for my opinion, because I've got to talk to you.

'I want to tell you straight that I'm against those two lying about here all day while I'm at work. I want you to remember that you've got a small child in the house and that Mavis and Tank are not setting a good example to her.'

My dad takes sugar and stirs his coffee. My mom tips her Cavalla and tries to say something, but my dad stops her with his raised hand. 'Wait, let me finish. You see, I don't want Gertie to get wise before her time. Look at the way she's talking already. And what d'you think the people are saying about that scarlet woman who's here all the time, rain or shine? Or,' my dad says, pointing his finger at my mom, 'have you ever thought what your father'd say about it?'

My mom jumps up very quickly. 'Jesus!' she says through her teeth, stubbing out her Cavalla in the saucer. '*You*, Piet van Greunen, you've got a fine cheek to bring up my father! All these years you've been calling him a hypocrite! A whited sepulchre whose trouser seat is worn out from sitting on the church benches!'

My mom looks quite ugly now. Her lips are drawn tight and thin. She speaks in a voice I don't know and that scares me. She stands behind her chair. '*You* . . .!' she shouts.

'Okay, okay!' my dad shouts back, pointing his teaspoon at my mom. 'I'm just telling you how I feel about the whole business, and I'm warning you tonight, Doris, the Lord is my witness, you'll live to regret it . . .'

'Shut up!' screams my mom, grabbing for her packet of Cavallas on the table.

'*You* shut up!' thunders my dad. 'Tell me, did you know Tank was a communist? Come on, tell me, did you know that?'

My mom sits down again, lighting another Cavalla. Her hands are trembling and she's breathing fast.

'Now *you* shut up, Piet, and let me talk,' says my mom and her voice sounds all right again. 'I've seen right through you. It's not Tank or Mavis that's the problem. The problem is you. You just can't stand seeing me have a bit of fun.'

'Ha!' says my dad.

'You can't take it that I enjoy myself. You begrudge me everything. You've got your job, your bladdie screws and your nails and your shit, you see people every day and meet new ones, but *me* you expect to stay at home day after day sitting on my backside.

'Look at the bladdie bad mood you're in when you get home at night and then you expect me to look into your long face too.'

My dad is getting short of breath now, but my mom goes on. She's terribly angry.

36

'What kind of a life d'you think it is?'

She turns to me and says, 'Gertie, go fetch your dad's pump.

'What do you think another woman would do in my place?' storms my mom.

My dad tries to say something, but he has no breath.

'I told you to go and get your dad's pump!' my mom shouts at me.

I jump up, and run to my parents' room and grab the pump on the bedside chest.

'I'll tell you what she'd do,' says my mom, 'she'd take her things and get the hell out of here!'

I give my dad the pump and he pushes the tubes up his nose. 'Scrrreech!' goes the pump.

'When you get home at night I'm here waiting, with Gertie bathed and clean and your food ready. And what do I get? Not even a grunt.'

'Scrrreech, scrrreech, scrrreech,' goes my dad's pump. He's pressing the ball faster and faster.

'Who's the bladdie fool in this house?' My mom presses her finger to her chest. 'Me!' she says. 'Me! Doris! *I'm* the fool. And why?'

'Scrrreech . . .' My dad is getting blue in his face and his eyes are turning red.

'Because I just scrape and bow to all clever Piet van Greunen's orders! Yes, Piet, no, Piet,' my mom says in that kind of a squeaky voice.

'Poor Doris . . .' she says.

'Scrrreech . . .'

'Her husband won't allow her anything, not even to make her own friends . . .'

My dad is now sitting right back, leaning his head on the back of the chair. I'm so sorry for him that I start crying.

Right on the spot my mom stops shouting. She gets up and pulls me towards her.

'It's all right, Mommy's little Gertie,' she says gently, but she's still angry. 'I'm going to take you out of this house. What kind of a life is this for a little baby like you? Poor little mite, your dad never even talks nicely to you, let alone take you to a merry-go-round.

'I should have listened to your grandpa. From the very beginning he said to me, "Dorothea," he said, "you should stay away from that Van Greunen chap. If you marry him he'll give you hell. I tell you, he's got a bad streak in him . . ."'

My grandpa is a tall man. Over six foot two, says my mom. He's an elder in Crawford and even goes to Synod sessions in Cape Town. My mom says he used to be a very strong man in his day. He could tear a telephone book in two with his bare hands.

Everybody calls him Uncle Hoppie. My mom says it's because he's so fond of rugby. Winter or summer, come wind or rain, every Saturday he's at Newlands. My mom says that's where my grandpa's health got a knock. He has terrible problems with his kidneys.

My mom says one moment it's as hot as hell at the rugby and the next moment it's as cold as a fridge. Actually that whole grandstand is one big draught. No wonder people get ill. And my grandpa doesn't want to go to the doctor with his kidneys. My mom says he doesn't believe in doctors. My grandpa says when your time's up it's up.

My grandpa comes to spend the last Friday of every month with us. He has to catch two trains – first one from Crawford as far as Maitland, then at Maitland he changes to a train for Parow. At Parow station he catches a bus to the Homepride bakery. Then it's only a little way from there, down Watering Street – three blocks – and then you turn up, towards Elsies, into Victoria Street.

Just before my grandpa turns up my mom hides away the ashtrays and the Cavallas. She also sucks Sen-Sen for her breath.

'Gertie,' she tells me, 'your grandpa will keel over just like that if he finds out I smoke. And I honestly don't know what he'd do if he heard about the bioscope. His heart will give in.

'So you won't tell Grandpa that Mommy smokes and ushers, will you, my girlie? You wouldn't like to send poor Grandpa to his grave, would you now?'

I stand up straight, my hands behind my back, shaking my head to and fro.

'And I think you'd better put away your cigarette sweets too. Grandpa wouldn't like it. He'll think you picked up the habit somewhere, or that you're mixing with bad kids.'

When my grandpa is here my mom changes all the way. She speaks with a thin slit of a mouth and she calls my grandpa Pai. 'Pai,' says my mom, 'Piet is really so sorry to miss you today. He's doing very well on the Railways right now.'

My grandpa calls my mother Dorothea and me Gertruida. 'Dorothea,' he says, 'I see they're adding on to the Catholic church up there.

Satan looks after his own all right. You must watch out that the child doesn't play in that neighbourhood. You know those Catholics . . .'

'Never, Pai!' cries my mom, holding her head kind of sideways.

After lunch my mom calls me. 'Gertruida,' she says in a very sweet voice, 'come and sing something for Grandpa. I've told him how lovely you sing.'

Then I stand in front of my grandpa, my hands behind my back, and I sing, 'Jesus loves me this I know', and 'When He cometh, when He cometh'.

My grandpa says, 'Mmmm', looking at me for a long time. 'She takes after the Prinsloos. She's got Magdalena's nose.' Then he takes a sixpence from his waistcoat pocket and gives it to me.

'No Pai, she doesn't only *take* after Magdalena! I think she'll also know her Bible as well as Magdalena did. You know, she can't get enough of David and Goliath, and Jonah and the whale. We have to tell it to her over and over again.'

At three o'clock in the afternoon my grandpa has to catch his bus back to the station, and then I must go to the bus stop with him and wait until the bus has gone. On the way to the bus stop he says, 'Gertruida, you must promise me you'll never play with Catholic children. If you do that you'll go straight to hell. The devil will roast you on a great fire and stick his fork into you.'

Nobody knows about me and my mom's secret with my grandpa. I mean about the Cavallas and the bioscope. When I come back from the bus stop my mom presses me against her and then she's the same as always. She laughs, and lights a Cavalla, and says, 'Oh, you're a clever one!' And she opens the kitchen dresser and takes out a handful of raisins and monkey nuts from a jar and gives them to me.

'Now come and help me peel,' she says. She gets going with the food. 'Your dad will be home soon. You can put the front plate on high for me.'

My mom sings while she works. 'Gertie,' she says, 'you're too young to understand yet, but I'm not really bad or wrong. I mean about your grandpa. Old people like your grandpa are just like that. To them smoking and bioscope are very sinful. Nowadays we know better, but so as not to hurt them we try to keep such things away from them. They'd be so terribly hurt if they were to find out, so we'd rather not tell them. You keep it a secret. It's better that way. You understand that, don't you?'

'Why doesn't Dad like Uncle Tank?'

My mom laughs. 'I suppose it's because he doesn't know Uncle Tank well enough. There's no harm in Uncle Tank.'

'Why does Dad say Uncle Tank is a communist?'

My mom laughs again. 'It's the war that made him like that.'

'But what's a communist?'

'It's someone like Uncle Tank.' My mom takes a cloth and wipes up the sink. 'He believes all the white and brown and black people are the same in the eyes of the Lord.'

My mom sits down at the kitchen table, lighting a Cavalla. 'Come to think of it,' she says, 'the communists may have a point there . . .'

PART TWO

O N THE SATURDAYS my mom does the matinée she takes me to
the Victoria bioscope with her. Then I put on my pink dress
with the frills, and my black patent-leather shoes with the bows on
the noses, and my white crocheted socks.

I'm allowed to sit upstairs, in the front row. My mom says that's
where the coloureds used to sit when they could still come to the
Victoria. They always kicked up a row and messed up the whole
place. People complained a lot, they said the coloureds spat on their
heads from up there. And you know the coloureds all have TB, my
mom says, so their spit is full of germs.

Everywhere on the stations and at the bus stops there's copper
plates with notices saying: Do Not Spit. £5 Fine.

But it's not because of the spitting that the coloureds can no longer go to the Victoria. My mom says it's because we've got a new government now, so the coloureds must go to their own bioscopes. The
Victoria is only for whites. It's *our* bioscope now.

Nowadays it's only the smart people, the ones with lots of money,
who sit upstairs in the bioscopes. I can sit there, says my mom, be-

cause the usherette's family are allowed to come to the bioscope for free once a month, and then they may sit wherever they like.

When the show begins I take a cigarette sweet from my packet, put it in my mouth, and start sucking, pretending to smoke.

At the matinées there's always a serial with cowboys and crooks. They fight all the time, chasing one another on horseback, and in the end it's the cowboys who win. It's easy to pick the cowboys out from the crooks, because the crooks have different hats. Right at the end, when the crooks are locked up, a man with a star on his chest appears on the screen and says, 'Crime doesn't pay!'

Once there was a serial I liked a lot. Spider Lady. She was really beautiful, and even though the pictures were black and white, you could see she had blonde hair and blue eyes, and she smoked with a cigarette holder. She lived under the floor of an old house among the cobwebs and drums with all kinds of things in them. Spider Lady gave orders to all the crooks to do bad things like stealing money and breaking into houses. The crooks went to her through a trap door, where she was sitting behind a desk with a telephone and lots of papers and stuff.

She also had a gun which she hid behind someone's wedding portrait. When she heard something, she'd quickly take out the gun and put it in her top drawer, with her hand right on it, ready to shoot if necessary.

In the end they caught Spider Lady too. Even though she was bad, I was rather sorry, because I liked her, perhaps because she looked just like my mom. She also swept her hair up like my mom. I'd have liked it better if Spider Lady had given up her bad ways and changed her life so she needn't have to go to jail.

After the serial there's a cartoon, a Mickey Mouse or a Tom and Jerry or a Popeye, and afterwards it's interval and all the lights go on.

Then I go down the stairs to where my mom stands near the screen with a tray full of ice creams and frozen suckers for the children to buy. She gives me a cup of ice cream, and after I've finished it I put another cigarette sweet in my mouth. Holding the packet in one hand I put my other elbow on it. And I suck on the cigarette and blow the smoke out through my nose like Aunt Mavis. The children gape at me and I glare back at them. I look at them the way my dad looks at the Jacobs kids.

There I stand smoking beside my mom until it's time to go back upstairs. I've seen a lot of pictures, and what I like best is *Tarzan the Ape Man* and *Nancy Goes to Rio* with Jane Powell in it. But the picture I like best of all is *Neptune's Daughter.* Esther Williams is in it and she's swimming and diving most of the time. That's really beautiful. I never knew one could swim so fast and dive from such high rocks.

That day after the bioscope I ask my mom to buy me a bathing costume like Esther Williams's and to teach me to swim and dive at Sea Point.

'We'll see,' says my mom.

I keep on nagging, saying 'But I *want* to swim!' because every time my mom does not really want to promise something she says, 'We'll see.'

47

After the matinée I wait for my mom in front of the Victoria. By that time all the people have gone, but I have to wait, because there's things an usherette has to finish before she can go home. When my mom does the matinée she needn't work in the evening too. Then it's her free Saturday and she stays home with my dad and me. I really like that and then I'm allowed to stay up late too.

In the twilight my mom and I go down to George's Café to wait for the Saturday *Argus*. Afterwards we – my mom and my dad and me – sit at the kitchen table, each with a piece of the newspaper. I get the comic with Henry in it, and Little Lulu, and Dagwood and Blondie.

Sometimes my mom and my dad read out bits from the newspaper to each other and then they talk about it for a long time.

Once my mom reads out a piece to my dad about some kaffirs who got on to the train at Langa station. Before they got in properly the conductor told them they were no longer allowed to sit in that part of the train, as it was for whites only now. The conductor pointed them to the very back of the train, the last coach, with the hard seats.

The kaffirs refused to listen and so they all got into the coach for whites and the train left.

When the train got to Cape Town station, the police were right there, waiting for them. As the kaffirs got out, they were caught one by one and taken to jail in the Black Maria. There was a whole lot of police so the kaffirs couldn't do anything, because the police had guns.

'Actually it's a disgrace, Piet,' my mom says after she's read it out.

'What disgrace?' shouts my dad. 'They're kaffirs and they're getting cheekier by the day. They got to be kept in their place. But you wait and see, Malan will teach them and the hotnots a lesson.'

'Ag shame on you, Piet,' says my mom, 'they're people too, you know.'

'People? Kiss my arse,' says my dad. 'It's a bunch of savages, is what they are. They got to be taught who's the boss in this country.'

'Why can't the kaffirs ride in our part of the train any more, Mom?' I ask.

'Because they cut the throats of white kids,' says my dad.

'Your dad's talking nonsense!' says my mom. 'I can't help feeling sorry for them.'

'Sorry my eye! They want to take over the country. I bet it's that Tank who's stuffed your head with all that twaddle again!'

One afternoon after the matinée I'm waiting for my mom at the Victoria again. She takes my hand and we go down the street. Near the Homepride she says to me, 'I don't feel like going home already. Anyway, old Cottage Pie is with your dad again. Why don't we go and have a look at what Uncle Tank and Aunt Mavis are doing?'

We turn round and start walking towards Watering Street. I suppose my mom doesn't feel like pretending to Cottage Pie, because she's still mad at my dad. Ever since they had the fight at the kitchen table that night they haven't spoken to each other again, and my dad has been sleeping in the spare room.

The morning after the quarrel my mom took the bottle of Radiant

Blue ink, dipped her finger into it and blotched my dad's face on the picture in the passage, the one of him standing by his engine. If you look at it quickly it's like a person without a head. I saw my dad looking at it when he came home that evening. But he said nothing, and he didn't wipe off the stain either, just left it like that.

It's not so good to be at home any more. My mom talks very little, except to Aunt Mavis and Uncle Tank, and when they come to visit she sends me out to play or to check if the hens have been laying. My dad works until late because they're taking stock at Woodstock Supplies, and when he comes home at night it's time for my mom to leave for the Victoria bioscope. Somehow I just know my mom and dad will only be friendly with each other again once that ink stain on my dad's face in the passage has been wiped off.

'Knock knock!' calls my mom at Aunt Mavis's front door, pushing it open further.

The room is full of smoke and it's kind of dark inside, so in the beginning one can't see very well.

'Doris!' says Aunt Mavis and comes to us. 'What a surprise!' She's wearing black pants and an old khaki shirt of Uncle Tank's. Her hair is covered with wavers.

Behind Aunt Mavis we can see Uncle Tank sitting at the table with another man. They get up and the man says, 'Come into my parlour . . .'

'You're just in time for a drink,' says Aunt Mavis, turning to call to Uncle Tank, 'Tank, get Doris a glass!'

The two men come towards us. 'Doris,' says Uncle Tank, 'I want you to meet a very dear friend of mine. Barnie Truter.' Then he turns to the man and says, 'Barnie, this is Doris. Just Doris.'

The man looks very handsome in a white suit with a navy-blue tie. When he smiles at my mom I can see that he has a gold tooth in his mouth. Actually he pulls up his lip in such a way that one can't miss it.

'He's a Dan Pienaar man,' says Uncle Tank. 'Eighth Division. El Alamein. They were heroes in our army, those boys. Doris, Mavis, remind me to tell you about it sometime.'

The man goes to stand right in front of my mom, hands on his hips, looking her up and down. Then he laughs and says, 'Hell's bells. And who have we here? It's Loretta Young's double, only a hell of a lot prettier!'

I can see that my mom is getting terribly embarrassed. She laughs, and looks down, and says, 'Ag come on!'

The Barnie man takes her hand, bends over and kisses it. 'I'm very, very pleased to meet you.'

Uncle Tank and Aunt Mavis burst out laughing. Right there on the spot I decide that I don't like this Barnie. If he tries to touch me, I swear, I'll bite him. Even so, I must say, he's very funny, kissing my mom's hand like that. And from that moment on she's just as pretty and as friendly as she used to be before she and my dad had that fight.

'Have a snort, sport,' Uncle Tank says to my mom, filling her glass. He holds the bottle up and says, 'White Muscadel. And Barnie says there's lots more where this comes from.'

My mom sits down on the chair Barnie has pulled out for her.

'I thought I'd just pop over for a minute to see what you folks are do-ing,' says my mom. 'I really can't stay. Piet is waiting at home.' She takes the glass and starts drinking.

'Let him wait,' says Uncle Tank. 'It'll do him good, the old bugger!'

Then, all of a sudden, I see something: a thing as big as a cat comes jumping from the window sill, right on Barnie's shoulder. A proper scare it gives me.

They all stop talking, turning to Barnie.

Only when the thing comes down from his shoulder to sit on his lap I discover that it's a small monkey.

'Ag shame!' I say, and the grown-ups burst out laughing. The mon-key presses its cheek against Barnie's stomach and starts fiddling with his shirt buttons.

'This is Pickles,' says Barnie, 'and he's the only one his master trusts with his secrets.'

'My goodness,' says my mom.

'I brought him back from up North.'

'Goodness,' my mom says again.

'Would you like to hold him?' Barnie asks me.

I hang on my mom's chair from behind, pressing my face into her shoulder.

'Don't be shy, Gertie,' says my mom. 'Answer the uncle when he talks to you, and take your finger from your mouth.'

'Oh, so her name is Gertie?' says the Barnie man. 'What a nice name. And such a pretty little girl too. Would you like to hold Pickles, Gertie?'

I nod.

'A monkey for Monkeyface!' laughs Uncle Tank.

Barnie gets up and holds the monkey out to me. I take him in my arms. He looks up in my face. His eyes are very round, and he stares at me very hard. But when I try to stroke him, he breaks away with a scream and jumps right across the table, back on the Barnie man's shoulder. He shuts his eyes tight and presses his face into Barnie's neck.

'Got a fright, did you, Pickles?' Barnie says to him. 'The little girl just wanted to hold you for a while.' Then Barnie looks at me and says, 'Don't you worry, Gertie, he'll get used to you just now. Come and sit here at the table and pretend you're not looking at him at all, then he'll soon come to you, you'll see.'

I sit down on a chair at the table with the grown-ups. Aunt Mavis brings me a glass of Oros. I drink it very slowly, in small sips, the way my mother takes her drink, glancing sideways at Pickles all the while. I take my packet of cigarette sweets from my pocket, take out one and start sucking it, my cigarette elbow resting on my other hand. I blow the smoke out through my nose.

The Barnie man stares at me for a long time. 'She's full of sights, this Gertie of yours, isn't she?' he says to my mom.

I can see the monkey peeping at me. After a while he cautiously slips down from Barnie's shoulder and sits on the table in front of him. Barnie offers him the glass of muscadel and he takes a sip.

They all laugh.

'Can you imagine?' says Aunt Mavis. 'He'll get a bellyache.'

I hold my cigarette sweet out to the monkey and he takes it, turning it over and over in his tiny black hands and staring at it for a long time before he sticks the wrong end into his mouth.

I laugh. 'Oh Mom, can't I have a monkey like this?' I clap my hands. 'Ag please, *please!*'

'Now the child's got a bee in her bonnet,' says Aunt Mavis.

'What will you do with a monkey?' asks Uncle Tank. 'You're a little monkey yourself. You're your Uncle Tank's monkey.'

I feel like crying. I throw my hands round my mom's neck, pleading, 'Please, Mommy . . .'

'We'll see,' says my mom.

After a while she gets up. 'We'd better go now,' she says. 'Piet'll start worrying.'

Barnie also gets up. 'Wait, let me take you home with the Hudson. I must skedaddle too. Date in Maitland.' He swings his bunch of keys and winks at Uncle Tank.

Barnie's car is parked in front of the house. It's a white car with a convertible roof. The monkey sits in front on Barnie's shoulder. I wish the Jacobs kids can see us riding in this smart car with the monkey.

When we get home my dad is standing in the front garden, watering the carnations. Old Cottage Pie must have gone home already. When my dad sees us getting out of the car, he turns off the tap and goes round to the back.

'Cheerio, Doris, Gertie,' says Barnie. 'We'll be in touch. Be good.'

My mom prepares the food and we sit down to eat. I'm itching to talk about the monkey, but no-one says a word.

Later in the evening, while my mom is washing the dishes in the kitchen, my dad comes past me in the passsage with the *Argus* under his arm. 'Gertie,' he says, 'who's that swank that brought you and your mom home?'

'It's Barnie Truter,' I say.

'Oh,' says my dad. 'Barnie. Imagine!'

'Oh well,' I say, 'he's got a monkey, you know.'

'Dorothea,' says my grandpa when he comes over, as usual, one Friday, 'it was your late ma's wish that when Gertie turns ten she must get fifty pounds. Gertruida is the first grandchild and she's named after Mai.'

'Ag shame, Pai,' says my mom and there are tears in her eyes.

My grandma died soon after I was born. She had diabetes and towards the end she was totally blind. There were pearls on both her eyes. My mom says she had a terrible temper, but she always kept her word and she was a very good Christian. In the big flu epidemic of 1918 she looked after all the sick people on the Cape Flats. She had no fear at all of catching the flu and came out of it as healthy as anything, just because her faith was so strong.

'Dorothea,' says my grandpa, 'I want to give you that money today. I know it's still a long time to go, but one can never tell what may happen and I don't know for how long I'll still be around.'

'What are you talking about, Pai?'

'I want you to take the money and buy Gertruida some Union Loan Certificates at the post office and put it away for when she really needs it one day.'

My grandpa looks tired and he walks like someone whose legs are aching.

'Don't you want to go to a doctor?' my mom asks quietly, taking my grandpa's hand.

'You know what I think of doctors, Dorothea. If a person falls ill it's God's will and you can't interfere with His ways. If your time's up it's up.'

'Ag, Pai.'

'Dorothea, you're my child. You're a Prinsloo, and before I go there's things I must know. Is everything all right between you and Piet? Are you keeping the Lord's commandments and bringing up this child in His name the way you promised when she was christened? As far as Piet is concerned, he's your husband for better or for worse and you've got to honour and obey him as the Scriptures command.'

I can see my mom is getting fidgety. She keeps clutching at the tablecloth. I think she's looking for her Cavallas.

'Ag Pai, don't get so upset. Relax. Every Sunday Gertruida goes to Sunday school with Koekie van der Merwe and she's learning to recite from the Bible. As for Piet, he looks after us all right. He's never raised a hand against me. Of course he has his ways, but that's because of the illness. No Pai, I can honestly tell you today there's many women who'd give anything to have a husband like Piet.'

My mom is talking fast and I can hear a hoarseness in her throat.

'Then I'm truly glad, my child. Everybody in your family is decent and upright and I don't want you ever to forget that. Now take your

56

grandpa Hendrik. He was a good man. An Afrikaner, a real Boer hero with fire in his blood. He never did anything without first consulting the Lord. Look at how many kaffir wars he survived, all because he had his faith.'

'No, it's true what you're saying, Pai.'

'And there's something else that bothers me. When I went outside just now I saw Gertruida playing at the fence by the chicken run with the child of those coloureds living there behind you. And I heard the klonkie calling her by her name just like he was her equal.'

'Ag Pai, you know how children are. They don't know about these things. But there'll soon be an end to it. The government's already given the coloureds notice: after the end of next month they won't be allowed to live here among us whites. Then they've got to find a place of their own, among their own kind. I suppose the Williamses here at the back will have to move out to Elsies River. I'm not sure. But one thing I can tell you: the ones living around here are a decent lot. They know their place, and they're quiet and everything. You hardly ever hear them. The mother and father are both teachers, I've heard.'

'I'm just saying, Dorothea. It's in the Bible, you know. Sheep and goats shouldn't mix. And you know what happened to Noah's offspring. We can thank the Lord for what Malan and his government have done. That man's head is in the right place. You won't find a more devout Christian and Afrikaner anywhere. He'll bring our people together again. I don't know, but with Smuts you can be sure everybody would have ended up marrying everybody else, a mixed heathen breed.'

'That's the gospel truth, Pai.'

'I mean, look at the Russians today. Every one of those commun-ists is a godless creature. They're all heading straight for the fire of hell.'

'That's so, Pai. Piet was saying just the other day that Joe Stalin is the Antichrist himself. Six six six and all that.'

'Piet may well be right for all you know. All the signs are there that the end is nigh. Revelations . . .'

While my mom is doing the dishes in the kitchen, my grandpa rests in the spare room. 'Grandpa has aged a lot all of a sudden,' says my mom. 'Have you noticed how slowly he walks nowadays? He isn't the straight tall man he used to be.'

It's as if my mom is talking to herself. 'Yes,' she says, 'when the end comes the old people can feel things.' And then she says, 'Gertie, take the dishcloth, put some Sunlight soap on it and go and wipe that ink stain from your dad's face in the passage.'

Railway people have lots of privileges, says my dad. They look after you when you're ill, there's a pension when you're old, and then there's the free pass and a special place at the seaside where you can go on holiday cheaply.

My dad says it's that top man in the Railways, Ben Schoeman, who's fought for his people. It's thanks to him that Afrikaners needn't take a back seat nowadays.

Once a year Railway people can have a free train ride anywhere in the Union. You can go as far as South West Africa or Rhodesia. On such long trips you can sleep for up to two nights on the train. They give you a compartment of your own and all you need to bring with you is bedding and food. No need to bother about coffee or tea, you can order that on the train. If you wish, you can even eat on the train. There's a special dining saloon at the far end. You go through, point out what you want on the menu, and the waiters bring it to you. But that costs extra, of course. You've got to pay for it.

The special holiday place for Railway people is at Hartenbos. They call it the ATKV resort. My mom and I were there in the last Christmas holidays and Aunt Mietjie and Uncle Koos went with. It's a long way, but not too far. You get on in the evening at Cape Town station and by the time you wake up in the morning you're nearly at Mossel Bay station. Then you can see the sea. The train stops there for a long time. My mom said they're shunting for Hartenbos. Then the train goes on, right next to the sea, and when you stop again it's Hartenbos.

There's already a man waiting in a lorry at the station. He knows you're coming because your seats have been booked months ahead and they've been told well in time on which train you'll be coming and at what time it'll arrive at Hartenbos. Then you get on the lorry with all your stuff, the man hands you a bunch of keys and a receipt, and takes you right up to the bungalow reserved for you.

That was the first time I ever slept on the train and it was really great to travel such a long way in our own compartment.

My mom and them were terribly jolly. Before the time she and Aunt Mietjie had prepared a chicken, and frikkadels, and cold potatoes and beet salad. We took it with us and ate a whole lot. A train ride works up an appetite, says my mom. All the way Uncle Koos sang and played on his mouth organ. He's very good with music and he can also play the accordion. Just by ear. I could have as many sweets as I wanted. My mom said it wasn't every day we had a holiday. The only thing was she didn't want me to come running to her if I got sick from all the sweets.

My mom made me a bed on a bunk on one side of the compartment and I fell asleep while the grown-ups were still talking and joking. When you lie like that, with your ear on the bunk, you can hear the wheels on the rails. It makes you sleepy and before you know what's going on you're asleep.

Once in the night I woke up from a commotion. I sat up and looked through the open slit in the window. Outside on the platform was a bunch of coloured kids, begging with cupped hands. The biggest one came up to the window and said to my mom, 'Some bread, please, merrim.'

'You have to dance for us first,' said Uncle Koos.

'Ag sis, man, Koos,' my mom scolded him, 'how would you feel if it was your child? At this time of the night, outside in the cold, and hungry?'

The boys started singing and dancing.

'Mietjie, isn't there some bread left in the food basket?' asked my mom.

My aunt passed bread and a handful of sweets and fruit to my mom to give to them through the window.

'Poor little things,' said Aunt Mietjie, 'just look at them!'

The train whistled to pull off again and the boys started fighting among themselves for the food.

'Those hotnots,' said Uncle Koos, 'fighting over everything.'

'It could have been *your* child,' said my mom. 'Have you thought of that?'

'A Boer can moer any hotnot up to maggots,' said Uncle Koos and started playing on his mouth organ again.

My aunt Mietjie looked sad. 'Koos can be so heartless,' she said to my mom.

It was a great holiday. The people were very jolly and at night they roasted bokkems on the coals and went on talking and singing and laughing till late. There were many kids to play with and one could stay out all day without being called by your mother. We splashed in the pools among the rocks, played hide-and-seek among the dunes, and collected lots of shells.

After their nap in the afternoon the old people came out for long strolls along the beach in the shallow water, the women with their dresses tucked into their navy-blue bloomers, the men with kieries.

One afternoon a man came round to the bungalows to say that on the Friday night there'd be a concert in the ATKV recreation hall next to the railway line. He had a small book in which he wrote down the names of all the people who could do something like singing, reciting, telling jokes or making music and who wanted to take part in the concert.

'When it comes to culture our people are a match for the English any day,' he said. 'There's lots of talent among the Afrikaners, only it needs to be developed. If everybody does his bit and we all stand together, the battle is already half won, because unity is strength. And *now* is the time for it.'

My aunt Mietjie pointed at Uncle Koos and told the man, 'He's wonderful with the mouth organ and the accordion. Both at the same time.'

'Ag no, Mietjie,' Uncle Koos objected, 'there's many who can play better than me. Why must you push me?'

The man seemed interested, and said, 'It's a team effort, Mister, and we need everybody, no matter how humble the contribution.'

Uncle Koos stood with his head hanging down. 'Ag man, I really don't know.'

'Now come on, Koos,' said my mom, 'why don't you play something?'

'Write down his name,' Aunt Mietjie told the man. 'That's the end of it. I'll see to it that he plays. His name is Koos Brits.'

'Well, all right then,' Uncle Koos said kind of shyly, 'I'll play for you, but only one piece, hey.'

'That's the stuff!' cried my mom, clapping her hands.

'But what will Mr Brits be playing? You see, the master of ceremonies has to announce it before the time.'

Uncle Koos looked at Aunt Mietjie, frowning.

'Red River Valley', said Aunt Mietjie.

The man shook his head. 'No, that won't do. It must be Afrikaans. It's an Afrikaner concert to promote our own culture.'

'Oh my goodness,' said Uncle Koos, 'now that's a thing for you.'

'"Aanstap rooies",' said Aunt Mietjie. 'Or "Boetie, sy's 'n perske-blom", or "Daar kom die wa" . . .'

'"Bolandse nôientjie",' tried my mom.

'That's it!' said Uncle Koos, snapping his fingers. '"Bolandse nôi-entjie" is the same as "Beautiful dreamer", so everybody will know it.'

'Done,' said the man, and he wrote it down and put the book in his shirt pocket. 'So then we'll be seeing each other at eight thirty on Friday night. All the best to you. God bless.'

There was a very big crowd in the ATKV hall on the night of the concert. It seemed as if all of Hartenbos was there. The hall was chock-a-block and they had to bring in more chairs. Two girls and two boys in folk-dance outfits showed us to our seats.

The hall was all done up with flags, and above the stage curtain was a huge poster. My mom read out the words: 'Afrikaners unite in the struggle.'

Uncle Koos was sitting next to me. He was very quiet and it seemed there was something wrong with his stomach because it kept on making noises.

A fat man with an awfully long beard went on the stage and everybody started clapping. The man held up his hand for silence and said a lot of things about culture and language and God and then all kinds of big words like what a privilege it was for Afrikaners to be together at such an auspicious occasion.

The man went on talking and he must have been getting on the people's nerves for after some time they started fidgeting and shifting about and clearing their throats. My mom also mumbled something about the unnecessary singsong, and can't you stop, for heaven's sake, so that we can begin?

At last the man said, 'We Afrikaners are a jolly lot, so why don't we ask the Camp Fire Brothers and their traditional boeremusiek band to open this concert with one of their lusty numbers.'

The curtain opened and five men in corduroys and neck scarves started off with the 'Askoek Seties'. Against the back wall were three ox-wagon wheels, painted red.

The crowd liked the music and started tapping their feet to the tune, laughing. Every now and then the man with the accordion shouted 'Yoohoo!' through the music and when the band had finished everybody shouted, 'More! More!'

The curtain was drawn and the fat man with the beard was back on the stage. 'Now as I said, ladies and gentlemen, we Afrikaners are a jolly lot, but it's time for something more serious. We are privileged to have in our midst tonight the famous singer Grieta van Breda who is going to sing for us an Italian aria from the opera *La Bohème*, accompanied by her equally famous mother, Mrs Van Breda.'

The crowd was very quiet. 'Who says our people can't do it?' asked the bearded man, and the curtain opened.

The Grieta woman was very beautiful and she wore a shiny, dark red tafetta dress. She sang very high notes and I rather liked it.

There was a baby who cried all the time and the children were shuffling on their seats. I don't think the people knew the song, because

64

they clapped at the wrong place. The one who drew the curtain sommer closed it while the woman was still singing. What I found rather
cute was a little girl in a long white dress standing beside the woman
who played the piano. Every now and then she turned the page of
the book from which the woman was playing.

After that an old man wearing a hat and braces played a very sad
song called 'The swallow' on a saw. Now that was something I'd never seen or heard before and I wondered whether it was a special kind
of saw and whether one could also use my dad's ordinary wood saw
in the garage for making music. The people liked that too and when
he'd finished they kept on shouting for more. But the man, looking
very angry, shouted back, 'No!' and jumped off the front of the stage
between two big vases with protea arrangements.

My mom said it was his artistic temperament.

Uncle Koos next to me never said a word. His stomach was carrying on something awful and I must say he looked very sick to me. I
also noticed that he didn't clap his hands once.

After the band had played another time there was a man telling
jokes, and barking like a dog, roaring like a lion and crowing like a
cock, and then came a woman who played 'Kom dans, Klaradyn' on a
harmonium. Then the bearded man said there would now be a short
interval of fifteen minutes and we could have ginger beer and cin-
namon biscuits in the lobby.

We went outside because Uncle Koos was complaining of the
heat. I went inside for more ginger beer and when I came back I saw
my mom and Aunt Mietjie holding Uncle Koos by the arms. He must

have been very upset about playing in the concert because I heard my mom telling him, 'Koos, you damn-well can't drop the people now!'

Uncle Koos tried to break loose, but my mom and Aunt Mietjie were holding him very tightly. His forehead was all shiny with sweat.

'Koos,' Aunt Mietjie said in a thin voice, 'if you leave here tonight, I tell you it's finished between us. You understand?'

The bearded man came to the front door and clapped his hands. We had to return to our seats, the concert was beginning again.

My mom and Aunt Mietjie took Uncle Koos back to their seats and sat down beside him. We kept on glancing at him. He was a very worried man.

Uncle Koos came on second. First, a short man in a black suit and tie was to recite something. He came on stage in short quick steps, then stopped in his tracks and stared at the fan in the middle of the hall. He stood like that for such a long time that everybody started turning their heads up to see what he was looking at, in case he was seeing something they weren't.

A vein was bulging on the man's forehead. He clasped his hands in front of him and started in a booming voice:

'Where is a night as black as this night?'

He sounded like someone who'd been badly hurt. In the hall everybody was deadly quiet.

'Where is a pain as deep as my pain?' shouted the man, even louder than before, and sounding as if he was going to cry.

Long after he'd finished his piece he still remained standing there, staring up at the fan on the ceiling. The people started coughing and the curtain was closed.

And then the master of ceremonies said, 'Our next item is "Bolandse nôientjie", played on the mouth organ and the accordion by Mr Koos Brits from Vasco in Cape Town.'

When the curtain opened Uncle Koos sat there with his accordion, and in front of him was the stand holding the mouth organ. Uncle Koos looked very lonely to me on that stage with all the flags and the proteas and the huge poster.

'Poor Koos,' Aunt Mietjie said to my mom, 'he looks like a fart lost in a storm of shit.'

My mom burst out laughing.

A woman with a thick grey bun behind her head and men's spectacles on her nose looked round angrily and said, 'Shhh!'

Uncle Koos began. A bit slow to start with, but it sounded all right to me. At first he only played the accordion, but when he got to the nice part he bent forward, curled his lips round the mouth organ and played on both instruments at the same time. It sounded beautiful.

Some of the younger people in the back of the hall started singing to the music. Uncle Koos liked that and began to swing the accordion to and fro with his body. More and more voices joined in and next to me my mom and Aunt Mietjie also started humming, because they know the words in English.

When he came to the end Uncle Koos refused to stop, so he started all over again. All told, he played it four times. Right at the end

Uncle Koos drew one finger to and fro across the keys, pulled the accordion open as far as it would go, and ended with a note that went on for a long time, ringing right through that whole big hall.

Uncle Koos took a bow, and by that time the people were jumping up and down, whistling and stamping their feet.

My mom shouted, 'Encore!' An elderly man in front of us turned round and snapped angrily at her, 'One doesn't say *encore* in Afrikaans. It's *herhaal!*'

'Barnie came round again yesterday, Doris,' says Aunt Mavis. 'He was asking about you.'

Aunt Mavis is standing in front of me with a skein of purple wool she's winding from my arms into a ball. I'm sitting on a chair with my back against the oven. Every time my mom bakes a cake I have to sit with my back against the oven, because the door doesn't close properly. It lets in air, says my mom, and then the cake falls flat.

'How come?' asks my mom from the sink, folding a cloth.

'He says he thinks you're a fine woman.'

I wave my arms up and down to keep up with Aunt Mavis's winding.

'Keep still, Gertie, the cake!' scolds my mom, and turns to Aunt Mavis.

'An old married woman like me?' She laughs.

'Barnie says if you weren't married he'd give you a go.' Aunt Mavis winks at my mom.

'Ag, go on!' My mom comes and sits with us.

'What's happened to his monkey? Has he still got it?' I ask.

'It goes with him wherever he goes.'

'Where'd he get the monkey, Aunt Mavis?' I ask.

'On one of his trips, I suppose.'

'But what's Barnie do, travelling around like that?' asks my mom.

'He's a travelling salesman. Irish linen. Goes all over the place. He's doing well. Heavens, Doris, did you know he was a Freemason? Wears the ring and everything. All those Air Force chaps are mos Freemasons or Sons of England. Those boys look after each other, that's for sure.'

My mom says nothing. The other day when my grandpa was here he said the Freemasons worship Mammon. Many of our Dutch Reformed people are also Freemasons and my grandpa said it was time they made up their minds. It's either the Church or the Freemasons. They're goat-riders, said my grandpa.

Aunt Mavis winds up the last bit of wool and sits down at the table opposite my mom. 'I hope the colour doesn't run. It's still wool left over from the war. I'd like to knit a Fair Isle cardigan for a change.'

The alarm clock goes off on the dresser. My mom jumps up and grabs the cloths. 'Oh goodness, the cake must come out. Scoot, Gertie!'

She takes out the cake pan quickly. 'Dash it all! Now I've burnt myself.' She turns the cake upside down on a wire stand on the table. 'My dad's coming over tomorrow and the old man is so fond of his bit of cake.'

'Smells good,' says Aunt Mavis. 'You going to ice it?'

'But isn't he married? Barnie, I mean.'

'That's another story,' says Aunt Mavis. 'While he was up North his wife left him. Just like that. For another man. A really pretty woman she was, I've heard. And English too. Just as well there aren't any children.'

My mom sighs. 'So we all have our ups and downs.'

'Tank says Barnie took it badly in the beginning. Started drinking quite heavily, you know. Barnie's wife, she's a fool, man. You know, Barnie has a house in Wynberg, all paid and everything. Quite a nice house with an indoor lavatory and an American kitchen. Some women are never satisfied.'

'One wouldn't say it, looking at him. He looks such a happy-go-lucky kind of person.'

'Yes,' sighs Aunt Mavis, 'we all have our secret sorrows. Now there's Caroline. In a month she'll be eleven. What's to become of her? On the seventeenth, that's her birthday, I want to go in for the whole day.'

'She may be better off than you think. At least she's among others just like her.'

'And next week there's the Moth Club dance. In Bellville,' says Aunt Mavis. 'Tank and I are going. I still have to find myself something to wear. I've swopped my Saturday shift with old Frieda Rose. She'll be working in my place that night.'

'Yes, and faithful old Doris van Greunen, mind you, is having a Saturday free; she'll be sitting on her backside at home, I suppose,' says my mom. 'Piet'll be in Touws River. He and old Cottage Pie got to take stock. You're a lucky girl, Mavis.'

'My goodness, Doris, thanks for reminding me! Why, you can go with us, man. As it is, we've been looking for a partner for Barnie that evening.'

'Never ever,' says my mom, pulling in her chin.

'Ag come on, Doris, be a sport, man. There's nothing wrong with it. Then we'll be two couples at a table and that's much more fun.'

'Piet'll kill me. And what about Gertie?' My mom lights a Cavalla.

'Piet needn't know, Doris. Why shouldn't you enjoy yourself now and then? And Gertie can stay with your sister for the night, can't she?'

'Gosh, I don't know.' My mom looks confused.

'Barnie's a good dancer, Doris. And another thing, people can say of Barnie Truter what they want, but he knows how to make a woman feel like a woman.'

'Let me think about it.'

'Doris, you may not think so if you look at him, but that Tank of mine is a first-class dancer, hey, stump-foot and all. It's just for the tango he has to sit out. A night out will do you and me a power of good. Come on, Doris, what d'you say?'

'What'll I wear?'

'We'll find you something.'

'I'll see,' says my mom, tipping off her ash into the saucer.

'Nonsense! You're going with. You listen to me, and that's the end of the story.'

I begin to cry, because I don't want my mom to go dancing with that Barnie man. 'I'm not going to stay with Aunt Mietjie!'

'See, now you've started something,' says my mom, scowling at Aunt Mavis.

'Sis, Gertie, how can you be so naughty? Don't you want your mom to be happy? Look at how hard she's working for you. Why can't she go out with me, only this once?' Aunt Mavis pulls my ear.

'If that man comes to our house I'll bite him!' I scream.

'Okay, okay,' says my mom. 'I'll stay home and watch how you sleep. That's what you want, isn't it? I'm not allowed my little finger's length of fun.' Now my mom's really mad at me.

'Ag sis, Gertie,' Aunt Mavis says again, 'that's not fair, man. Your poor mother.'

My mom stubs out her Cavalla. 'Let's have a drink, Mavis. Some days I also feel like getting drunk.' She gets up, takes two glasses from the dresser and fetches my dad's rum from the sideboard in the front room.

'You're better off, Mavis,' she says when she comes back. 'Look at me, with a man like Piet. And now even my own child is bossing me around.' She pours the glasses half full and takes a gulp.

'Before we were married, Piet took me out a lot. There was no end to what he'd do for me. One present after the other. And look at how things have turned out. I was talking to Piet about it just the other night and d'you know, Mavis, he had the cheek to say, "But you don't feed a fish worms after you've caught it, do you?" "Funny," I told him, "bladdie funny, ha ha!"'

Aunt Mavis sips her drink and says to me, 'Gertie, look at me. Come on. Look me in the eyes, there's something I want to tell you.'

I look at her.

'If you let your mother go with me and Uncle Tank to the Moth Ball, I'll ask Barnie to get you a monkey too. That's if your mother says it's all right.'

I jump up. 'Oh Mom, can I have a monkey? Oh please, Mom, please, ag please . . .!'

'We'll see,' says my mom. She looks out in front of her, pushing one of the purple wool balls to and fro on the table with her finger.

'I have a little black dress in my wardrobe which I've only worn once,' says my mom. 'You haven't seen it. It's got a sweetheart neck, you know, and then it's cut low across the hips with a bow on the side, and a marcasite brooch.'

'I was also thinking of black,' says Aunt Mavis. 'It goes with everything. One can't go wrong with a black dress.'

'But I'll have to try it on first. I'm not sure I can still fit into it. And I'll have to hang it out for the smell of the moth balls. Bring your drink, I'll show it to you.'

We go through to my mom and dad's bedroom. My mom digs into the back of the wardrobe, pulls out a box and takes the dress from it. She holds it up against the window.

'Gee, but that's really smart, Doris!' cries Aunt Mavis. She sits down on the double bed. 'If we were one size I'd have taken it over from you.'

My mom takes off her clothes and pulls the dress over her head.

'Streamline!' says Aunt Mavis. 'Black always makes one look thinner. No, I tell you, Doris, you're fixed up. Now it's only me who's got to find something for this old body.'

It's a long dress with a long narrow frill right down to my mom's ankles. The bow which holds the brooch in place is covered in sequins.

'You look just like the Spider Lady, Mom!'

'You look ten years younger, Doris.'

My mom poses in front of the tall mirror to look at herself. She lifts up one arm. 'I'll have to take it in a bit under the arms, otherwise my bust bodice will show. I must have lost some weight.'

We go back to the kitchen where my mom pours some more rum for herself and Aunt Mavis. 'I really don't know *what* will happen if Piet ever finds out.' She's wearing the long dress and sits holding her legs together to one side.

'Ag, come on, Doris. You can tell him later, after the dance. I'm sure he won't say anything. It's all innocent.'

'What'll I tell Mietjie?'

'Think up something. There's more than enough time.' Aunt Mavis empties her glass and gets up. 'Well, got to go. So it's all right now, isn't it, Doris? We're going to the dance on the fourteenth? Can I tell Barnie?'

'All right, if you insist.'

Aunt Mavis turns to me. 'Now you've heard it all, Gertie, haven't you? Your mother's going dancing and you shut up. Not a word to your father. Not to anybody. You swear?'

'Let the child be, Mavis. I'll talk to her.'

'Gertie, you heard, hey?' Aunt Mavis says again. 'You say a word to anybody and it's tickets! No dice. No monkey. You got it?'

Sometimes my mom allows me to sit in front of our house on the pavement, by the gate. I may also walk to the end of the block, but only on the pavement on our side. I'm not allowed to go into the street. Sometimes, if there's someone with her, she also sends me to sit at the gate and watch what's going on in the street.

Once my dad found me there on the pavement and asked, 'What're you doing out here in the streets? Go inside. The kaffirs will catch you.'

He scolded my mom: 'Doris, I don't want the kid to hang about in the streets. She's seeing things she's not supposed to see and before you know where you are she'll be just like the scum around here.'

I've discovered that my mom sends me out to the gate when she and the people visiting her want to talk about things I'm not supposed to hear.

One afternoon Uncle Tank turned up at our house on his own. He was very grumpy and he didn't even greet us. He just stopped in the kitchen door and said, 'Doris, I want to talk to you. It's about Mavis and Caroline. Mavis wants to take the child back in with her.'

Then Uncle Tank looked hard at me and my mom sent me to the gate. 'But stay out of the streets, you hear! You heard what your dad said.'

The school was just coming out and the kids were coming up from way down Victoria Street. When they came nearer I saw them stopping at the corner in front of old Uncle Wilson's gate. After a while some grown-ups joined them. From the house, a block lower down in the street, on the opposite side of Watering Street, two women in aprons and slippers came hurrying towards the others. It was Mrs Kleijn and her mother, old Mrs Kleijn.

Old Uncle Wilson was standing among the others with his hat on his head, and he kept on pointing with his kierie at something on the ground. Soon there were so many people and kids around that one couldn't see him any more.

I got up and walked along the pavement as far as Uncle Wilson's house and then pushed through the crowd until I was right beside him. On the ground was a long brown snake which Uncle Wilson said he'd found in his hedge and killed with his kierie.

I first got a fright when I saw the snake, but it soon passed because I could see it was really dead. It couldn't do anything, otherwise those people wouldn't have been standing there like that.

Old Uncle Wilson was telling the story over and over, because all the time there were new people turning up who also wanted to hear about it.

'Man, I was standing there on the stoep when I saw a piece of paper lying there by the hedge. You know how I am about litter in my yard. So anyway, I got up to go and pick it up and throw it in the bin and just as I was bending over, out of the corner of my eye, I saw something moving. At first I thought it was a rat or something and I picked up the piece of paper, you see. But then I saw the eyes. Small, yellow-green, shiny eyes, moving to and fro in the thing's head. And as it came closer I said to myself, "But rats don't behave like this!" Well, and then everything happened so fast that I'm still not sure, but those were a snake's eyes and the next moment it was right there in front of me. And it reared up, all the way. It came right up and cupped its head, ready to strike.'

Old Uncle Wilson cupped his hand like a snake's head and said, 'Ssss . . .' The kids pulled back. 'As luck would have it I had my kierie with me, otherwise I don't know. So I held it like this, in front of my chest.' Old Uncle Wilson held the kierie in both hands to show us.

'Gosh, Uncle, and what happened then?' asked Karel van der Merwe.

'No, as I said, I held the kierie like this, and that was something this child of Satan didn't expect, you see. It pulled back, but by now it was really mad. Its tongue was flicking to and fro as it made ssss . . . louder and louder.'

'Oh God, it gives me the creeps,' Karel's mother said, shivering. She's come out into the street just as she was, her hair full of dinkies. 'You sure the thing's dead?' she asked.

'Ag yes, Mynie, dead as a doornail, man. Now I tell you,' old Uncle Wilson went on, 'I know this kind of snake – it's a cobra, you see – he spits you in the eyes, and when that happens to you you're blind on the spot. You can rinse your eyes in Dettol or whatever, you can pray, you can send for the doctor, you can do what you want, but it's no use. Everybody will just shake their heads and tell you there's nothing they can do for you. If a cobra spits at you, you stay blind till kingdom come.'

'So what happened then, Uncle?' asked one of the children.

'Well, to make a long story short, I turned my head sideways, you see. So the cobra couldn't spit me in the eye. But before I turned my head I took a good look to see exactly where he was. Then I flicked round my kierie to grab it by the bottom end, and with the crook I hooked him round the head and gave him one hell of a jerk. At the same time I jumped out of the way so the snake wouldn't land on top of me, you see. You know, this kind of cobra is quick, man – they say it strikes at thirty miles an hour. And when the snake was down on the ground like that I had my foot ready and I was holding the kierie by the handle again.'

Old Uncle Wilson leaned forward with his foot raised from the ground, striking with his kierie. 'And I stamped down! I was thinking by myself, you devil, today it's you or me. Once you've got him down like that, your foot on his neck, a snake is helpless. So I took aim with my kierie and gave him one, two, three, I don't know how many blows on the head. But that snake refused to die. His tail was curling right round my ankle.' Uncle Wilson pointed at his leg. 'Right there!' he said.

'Oh God, not for me, thank you!' cried Mrs Haasbroek.

'Then I saw a brick. Wait, I thought, and I picked it up and I started hammering. I hammered with all my might, and this time I could see it was working, because there was black blood spurting all over the place. And I kept on hitting and hitting it until I was quite sure it was dead.'

Old Uncle Wilson bent over, picked up the snake by its tail and held it up in front of him.

The people got scared and stood back.

Old Uncle Wilson put the snake down again. 'He must be more

than six feet, I think. But my ruler is somewhere inside; I still have to go and look for it. So here's the devil, its head bruised like the Bible tells us to do.'

'Its mate is going to come and look for it tonight to take revenge,' said old Mrs Kleijn. 'I've read somewhere that snakes do that.'

The kids all moved away from the hedge, very quickly.

'Ag balls,' said old Uncle Wilson. 'If it's dead it's dead.'

'Yes, but you'll have to chop it up in bits, otherwise the life will come back into its body,' said Maizie Vlooi who'd also joined us. 'I've heard that for the honest truth.'

'Suppose the whole street is full of snakes?' said young Mrs Kleijn. 'All the while, as we're going about our business, sleeping in peace and whatnot, there's a whole brood of them slithering among us.'

'One ought to get the municipality to come and clean up the place,' said Mrs Haasbroek.

'What're you worrying about?' said old Uncle Wilson, laughing. 'You womenfolk are mos fond of snakes.'

'Shame on you,' said Karel's mother. 'Mind your tongue, Uncle.'

Down the street Gregory's dad was coming up towards us carrying a school satchel. The people saw him and fell silent.

'They'll be moving out one of these days, won't they?' said a woman with a large mole beside her nose.

'Once the hotnots are gone property prices will start going up again,' said the young Mrs Kleijn. 'For all you know it's in their yard the snakes are hatching. Such a filthy lot.'

'I have a good mind to give him his snake and tell him, "Here you are, Williams. See, we've already started cleaning up the place, so you needn't do it when you leave"',' old Uncle Wilson said angrily.

Gregory's dad had reached the corner. He didn't look at us. He turned off into Watering Street, going towards Alexandra Street.

'Stuck-up too,' said Mrs Toerien. 'Isn't that just like them? Don't even greet decent folk.'

My mom and I went to the station to see my dad off to Touws River. All the way my mom was holding his hand, talking to him in her nice voice.

'You got your pump, Piet?' she asked. 'Maybe you won't even need it over there. They say the Karoo air is like free medicine. Remember to take your Olino every night for your lungs and I put in your maroon pullover in case it gets cool in the evenings. You'll see there's a clean shirt for every day. You sure you'll be all right on your own?'

My mom spoke nonstop. 'And Piet,' she said as we went past Visser's shoe shop, 'when you come back we really should take the car one Sunday and drive out to Campers Paradise for the day. You're killing yourself, working like this all the time. It'll do you a world of good. The change, the rest, the fresh air, ag man, just getting away from it all for a bit.'

My mom was specially good to my dad the week before he left for Touws River. Perhaps it was because she'd be going with Uncle Tank and Aunt Mavis to dance with that Barnie man and my dad couldn't go with. I took care not to say anything to my dad about it. Somehow I just knew he wouldn't like it. I sommer knew he'd be sad. And then there was the monkey too, which I wouldn't get if my dad found out. So I felt very sorry for my dad at the station, and I think my mom did too. Before the train pulled off my dad put his hand in his pocket and gave me a tickey.

'Don't buy chewing gum with this, you hear, it's full of germs. And be a good girl now, listen to your mother and keep off the streets.' Before my dad left my mom had baked him some pumpkin fritters because he likes them so much. I think she was feeling bad about the dance.

My mom told Aunt Mavis one morning she wasn't sure whether the dance was such a good idea. She didn't like doing things behind my dad's back. 'After all, Piet's still my husband, you know.'

'What he doesn't see he won't know about,' said Aunt Mavis, and once again she made my mom change her mind.

'Actually I'm worried. You know, it's as if Piet *can't* enjoy himself any more. Mavis, the accident has changed that man a lot. If you'd known him before the time you wouldn't think it was the same man.'

'You're panicking too much, Doris. It'll be all right again, but things like that take time and you're too impatient.'

'It's as if Piet's got something on his mind,' my mom said, fetching the bottle of rum from the sideboard. 'If only he'd *say* something, but he doesn't.'

'I told you men are like that. They can't show their feelings. Take Tank now. He may look all don't-care, but I know he's suffering.'

'Why must one have so much trouble?' asked my mother and took a sip of rum.

In a high voice Aunt Mavis started singing 'Ah, sweet mystery of life'. And then she said, 'Now you stop worrying, Doris van Greunen. You worry, you die; you don't worry, you also die, so why worry! Just take things as they come and make the best of them. Cheers!'

'You must be right, but I really can't help it . . .'

'You see, there you're off again! You sound just like an old woman.'

'Yes, but . . .'

'Stop it!'

'All I meant to say . . .'

'I give up,' said Aunt Mavis, and she got up and took her Cavallas. 'I'm going, before I start crying along with you!'

I went to sit on my mom's lap and told her to better make sure she was going to dance with that Barnie man, otherwise I wouldn't be getting my monkey.

My mom laughed, pressed me tight against her and said, 'I wish I could have been more like you, my little Gertie. Small as you are, you're already a little chancer.'

'Dad'll like the monkey when he comes back. It'll make him laugh a lot, because people can't help laughing at a monkey, they're so *funny.*'

'Funny, hey, *funny!*' my mom teased me, and lifted up my dress to tickle my tummy. 'Now would you like a piece of cake?'

While my dad is in Touws River I spend the nights with Mrs Kok opposite. My mom says it's a comfort to her that it's so close, especially when she has to work in the evenings. And she doesn't want to bother

Aunt Mietjie every time. That would also mean taking the bus to Plywoods where Aunt Mietjie lives. Aunt Mietjie has a life of her own now, and she and Uncle Koos are engaged. They didn't get engaged with a ring, says my mom, but with a bedroom suite. It's better that way, she says, what with life getting more expensive all the time. It's tough on young people who got to set up a new house.

Mrs Kok is a bit deaf and one's got to speak up. Her husband is a guard on the Railways and he works night shift. People call him old Kok Bok, because they keep a goat in their back yard.

I rather like sleeping over at Mrs Kok's, because she always has something nice in her house and every evening before we go to bed she gives me a small mug of warm goat's milk to drink. We sleep together in one bed, which is a big four-poster with frills round the canopy up above. My mom says every time she thinks of the two of us in that big bed she can kill herself laughing. If there's one thing she'd love to see it's me and Mrs Kok in the four-poster.

Mrs Kok keeps all the windows of the house closed because of the skollies. 'They'll steal the very teeth from your mouth,' she says every evening as she closes the windows. 'They spray stuff through the windows which makes you fall into a very deep sleep and then they ransack the place. When you open your eyes in the morning there's nothing left. Even the bed is gone from under you.'

Mrs Kok wears a turban round her head. It's to hide her grey hair, my mom says.

'You know what old Kok Bok told me the other night while I was watering the front garden?' my dad once said. 'He says his whole pay goes into snuff. The old girl believes that snuff will clear her ears, but the less it helps the more she takes. He says there's so many empty tins of Singleton's in that house, she can pave the whole yard with them.'

My mom had a good laugh. 'Ag, but she's a good old soul and she loves kids. You must see how she fusses about Gertie. Always asks about her and every now and then she sends over a small pail of goat's milk, specially for Gertie.'

There's a big painting in Mrs Kok's sitting room. One never gets tired of looking at it, and every time you look you see something different.

In the middle of the picture is a broad river. On one side of the river there's a lot of men and women with ox-wagons and bushy things that look like hedges. The men are wearing old-fashioned hats and the women kappies. In between the hedges the men are shooting with their guns.

On the other side of the river there's a hill and a whole crowd of near-naked kaffirs coming running over the hill. A lot of the kaffirs are already shot dead and they've fallen into the river. The river is red with blood.

Mrs Kok says it's the Battle of Blood River and the whites on the one side are Voortrekkers. Those people, the Voortrekkers, are all ours. They're Afrikaners who believed in God.

The Voortrekkers killed the kaffirs because they'd knocked the white children's heads to bits against the wagon wheels and dug out their insides with the spears.

When they murdered the kids like that, says Mrs Kok, the Voortrekkers prayed to God and promised Him that if He'd help them to kill the kaffirs they'd keep that day as a Sunday every year.

So God helped the Voortrekkers, says Mrs Kok, and that's why the government are now putting all the kaffirs on one side. So that they won't kill the white kids again. If ever they find a kaffir in the streets after dark, says Mrs Kok, they put him in jail there and then.

'But why are they sending the coloureds away too?' I ask her.

'Those hotnots are half kaffir,' says Mrs Kok. 'They've got the same heathen blood in their veins. You better watch out for the hotnots. They can put up a straight face in front of you, but when it gets dark they steal up from behind and stab you in the back with a knife.'

'And the Williamses? They're not like that. They're whiter than most other coloureds and their hair is straight too.'

'My girlie, those whitish ones, the ones who always put on airs, they're the worst of the lot, because one never knows for sure about them. No. A hotnot is a hotnot and he'll always be a hotnot. It's those half-white ones who are particularly dangerous. They spur on the others. And they breed like vermin.'

Aunt Mietjie and Uncle Koos are to collect me on the night of the dance. My mom's arranged with Aunt Mavis not to come and pick her up before I'm gone, and then they'll all meet up with Barnie at the Moth Club. She doesn't want me to sleep over at Mrs Kok's that night. 'Just in case. You know how people are. All those filthy minds.'

My mom has her hair done specially at Nola's in Main Road. After she's made up her face she turns the side mirrors of the dressing table so that she can see her hair from the back.

Then she takes a pencil and makes a beauty spot below one eye. She looks at herself in the mirror for a long time.

'Who do I look like, do you think?' she asks me.

'Like Spider Lady.'

'Is she pretty?'

'Ye-es, but not as pretty as you.'

My mom laughs and puts a bit of her Evening in Paris behind my ears. 'My little girl's growing up,' she says, and stands up in front of the tall mirror. She turns round to check her legs to see whether the seams of her stockings below the hem are straight.

'Dad says that Barnie man is a swank.'

My mom turns round quickly to me and asks, 'Since when does your dad know about him?'

'The other evening. Dad was in the front garden when he dropped you and me at the gate.'

'Oh,' says my mom. She's quiet for a long time, and then she says, 'Perhaps he is a swank for all you know.'

'Well, *I* thought he was a swank.'

My mom laughs. 'What do you know about swanks? You're just talking. Just like your dad. And don't talk about "that Barnie man", why can't you say Uncle like I told you when you're talking about grown-ups?' She takes her shiny evening bag. 'I wonder what's keeping Aunt Mietjie?'

We go through to the sitting room. There we sit down. My mom puts on a record and lights a Cavalla.

'I wonder what your poor dad's doing all on his own tonight. I hope they're giving him proper food to eat. There's Aunt Mietjie, I've just heard the gate. Go and open the door.'

Aunt Mietjie gapes at my mom when she sees her in the evening dress. 'All dressed up!' she cries, standing back. 'What's the occasion?'

My mom gives a funny laugh. 'Ag, this is sommer an old dress. It's been hanging in my wardrobe for years. I thought I should try it on again. No, it's just some friends taking me out, man. Old friends, you know. They're taking me out for the evening so we can talk about the old days.'

PART THREE

ONE MORNING MY MOM AND I catch the train in to Cape Town for shopping. We're dressed in our best clothes. Christmas is just around the corner. Railway people get their pay early so they can get everything ready for Christmas. It's an expensive business, says my mom, but what can one do? Some years you go on paying for up to three months afterwards for all the stuff you had to buy to keep everybody happy. It's presents for everybody and eating from morning to evening. And everyone who comes to visit has to have a drink. You've got to decorate the house and then there's Christmas crackers and tips for the postman and the rubbishmen and you just keep on dishing it out, because you want them to have a happy Christmas too.

Every year she promises herself *this* is going to be a quiet Christmas, but it never works out like that. One really ought to put away money through the year for Christmas, says my mom, but there's always something that comes up for which you've got to take out your purse.

Sometime between Christmas and New Year you're already broke.

On Boxing Day it's Campers Paradise and that means she has to stay up till all hours to prepare the cold meat and boil the beetroot for salad.

On New Year's Eve it's the Outspan Hotel where you dance into the New Year and celebrate with your friends and it all costs money. One doesn't want to miss it either, because you never know whether you'll all be together again next year. It's an ungodly hour by the time you get home and then it's January first and the whole house is turned upside down and in a mess and already there's new visitors to be seen to. They've hardly gone when it's time to get ready to go to the Green Point Pavilion because now it's the Coon Carnival, and she won't be missing that for anything, not a damn.

In between she's got to usher for a midnight show and heaven knows what, and when at last it's all over she can only thank God. This year she wants to make sure she gets a rest in between. It's all right for Aunt Mavis to say she's complaining unnecessarily because Aunt Mavis can sit back like a lady while Tank fetches and carries. He even makes the food. She needn't even put her own batteries into her bioscope torch.

My dad is back from stocktaking and he's got it just as good, says my mom, because that bunch of men at the stores have been party-ing now for heaven knows how long. In the evenings he's barely fin-ished eating at home before old Cottage Pie turns up to take him for a quick one at the Central Hotel. And so it goes on, day after day, she's all flaked out already and it's not even Christmas yet.

And *this* Christmas, says my mom, my dad'll be going with her to my grandpa's even if she has to drag him there. It's a shame, going to Grandpa every year on her own, always having to find an excuse for my dad.

'He doesn't speak to your grandpa, you know,' she says. 'It's a disgrace. Grandpa is old and sickly. Christian people don't do this kind of thing. They got to make up. One of these days your grandpa will be in his grave, and how's your dad going to live with his conscience then?'

On Christmas morning, says my mom, we're going to Crawford in the Plymouth and no two ways about it.

Aunt Mavis says my mom gets too worked up. She's got to relax. No point in getting old before one's time. Before you know where you are you're in your grave and what have you had of your life? 'Now come on, can you tell me that, Doris?'

'I can't be like that,' says my mom. 'A person's got a responsibility.'

'Yes, but you can make such a singsong about everything. Take it easy, man.'

'You must remember I've got a child too. I must set an example.'

'There are times I really don't understand you, Doris. You can be such a good sport. Look at that night at the Moth Ball. You were so jolly, you looked beautiful and one could see you were enjoying yourself. And then suddenly, the very next day, you're like you are now. All holier-than-thou and full of shit. You're always moaning about Piet, but you're just as bad.'

We get off at the station. My dad is already waiting for us under the big clock. There are two men with him. 'Doris,' he introduces my mom, 'this is Fight, and this is Cole. Remember, I've told you about them. I told Fight and Cole they should bring over their little wives to our place one Sunday afternoon.'

My dad has a jolly look on his face. He's not like that at home. The two men shake my mom's hand. 'Merry Xmas,' they say. The one my dad calls Fight has a long, twisted moustache.

'And this is my girlie,' says my dad, picking me up. He takes me to a machine in the station, pushes a penny into the slot, and it pushes out a chocolate. 'Here's a chocolate for you,' he says and kisses me. He's had a drink, I can smell it. 'Now what'd you like for Christmas?'

My dad puts me down again and gives my mom his pay envelope. 'Well, Doris, we've got to get back to work. We've just come through in Fight's car. You buy yourselves something, but keep an eye on the money. Make sure the child's with you so she doesn't get lost, and watch out, the skollies are on the lookout again. Every bladdie hotnot in the Cape is on the streets today.'

My mom's bad mood is gone. She laughs, holding my hand. 'Let's take a short cut across the Parade to Plein Street. One can find almost everything you need at the CTC.'

'When is Uncle Barnie bringing my monkey, Mom?'

'Gertie, I don't want you to set your heart on it for Christmas, hey. Barnie first has to find a monkey, you don't find them here in the Cape and he'll only be on the road again after New Year.'

'Pity. I thought we could buy a present for the monkey.'

There's a Father Christmas at the CTC Bazaar. My mom and I stand watching him for a while, and he gives me a blue balloon and my mom buys me a lucky dip from him. He tries to pick me up, but I pull away.

'Ag no, Gertie!' says my mom.

'Let's go. There's a man under those clothes. It's not a real Father Christmas.'

'Now what makes you think that?'

'Grandpa said so. He says the grown-ups are always telling lies to kids.'

'Perhaps you're getting too big for Father Christmas,' my mom says after a while. 'Come, we've got lots to do. I need some lace from Spracklens too. Will you remind me?'

All day long we walk along the streets, from one shop to the next. I'm trying to figure out how long I'll still have to wait for my monkey, and I wish we can go and sit in the Gardens for a while so I can check what's in my lucky dip. My new shoes are chafing my heels. My mom buys me a whisk with crinkle paper streamers which one's supposed to wave, and I have my hands full with the dip and the whisk and the balloon. My mom has also stopped once, her hand on my shoulder, to take off one shoe and complain about her feet.

'Ouch!' She puts the shoe on again. 'The Cape is so crowded today. Let's go to St George's Street first, then we can have something to eat at the Waldorf.'

I like the Waldorf a lot. It's a huge place with lots of tables. My mom says it's a restaurant and if you eat here you'd better mind your manners and use the right knives and forks, or else the people will glare at you and wonder what kind of house you come from.

The waitresses serving at the tables all wear black dresses with white lace bonnets on the backs of their heads and white lace pinafores. They're all white girls. And they only speak English. My mom says that's how it is in the Cape. She gives our order in English too. For me she orders a steak and kidney pie with gravy and a banana split, and a mixed grill and tea for herself.

A group of people go up to the stage in front and start making music. It's rather nice. My mom says it's Strauss waltzes they're playing. The man who wrote the music was called Johann Strauss.

'He wrote the most beautiful waltzes,' says my mom. 'If you listen properly you can hear birds singing in his music. He heard the birds as he drove through the Vienna Woods with his girlfriend in a coach.

'Oh, he loved that woman! He wrote his music specially for her and then they danced to it – he in a black tuxedo and a bow tie, and she in a wide white dress. They ballroomed on the floor, looking into each other's eyes.'

'How d'you know, Mom?'

'They made a picture of Johann Strauss's life. I saw it. *The Great Waltz*. If it comes back I'll take you there.'

'And what happened then?'

'Things didn't work out for him, and he had to say goodbye to her and then she went away.'

'Why? Why didn't things work out for him?'

'Ag, I can't remember the story so well any more, but Johann Strauss led a helluva life after that. All artists have a hard time. Just you watch. They have terribly sad lives, all of them.'

'But why?'

'That's how it is with artists. They're not born to be happy.'

'What's happiness, Mom?'

'Eat your pie, it's getting cold.' My mom lights a Cavalla and blows the smoke into the air. 'Happiness,' she says, getting all sad herself. 'If you had it once you keep on looking for it for the rest of your life, but it never lasts long.' She looks out in front of her and then she says, 'Happiness is something that just happens to one. One day you wake up and you do the things you always do, and you meet someone and suddenly, suddenly there's this feeling inside you. You sommer want to laugh and cry, all at the same time, and you feel like doing something great, something nobody else can do, but you can't do anything and you don't know how to either. That's what happiness is, that's what it means to be happy.'

The orchestra finishes its tune. A man in evening clothes takes a bow and everybody claps. The man turns round, gives a sign with his stick, and the orchestra starts playing again.

'Just listen, how lovely,' says my mom. 'Isn't it beautiful? Johann Strauss had to choose between his love for music and his love for a woman.'

I'm busy on my banana split when I suddenly see that Barnie man. He's standing behind my mom's chair, covering her eyes with his two hands.

My mom gets a fright, but then she smiles. 'Who's it?'

'Guess.' He looks at me, winking, and pulling a face to show that I mustn't tell her. He also pulls his mouth in such a way that one can see his gold tooth.

'Prince Charming.'

'How'd you know?' Barnie laughs, takes his hands off my mom's eyes, pulls out a chair and sits down with us. He's dressed very smart indeed, a dark green suit with a double breast and a cream shirt and a pale green tie. He's handsomer than my dad, I think, much thinner and taller, with his brown half-curly hair.

And they're both very jolly.

'Christmas shopping?' asks the Barnie man. 'Gosh, Doris, but you look beautiful!' He pretends he's going to whistle and my mom's whole face lights up.

'And what about you, Monkeyface? Enjoying your split?' he asks me.

He's also calling me Monkeyface now, like Uncle Tank, and I don't like it one bit. I'm not his Monkeyface and I feel like telling him so, only I don't want to lose that monkey.

'Where's Pickles, Uncle Barnie?'

'In his cage at home.'

'Must he stay in a cage then?'

'Yes, otherwise he'll run away or get stolen.'

'Monkeys must stay in cages,' says my mom. 'They're not people, Gertie. Now put that monkey out of your head.'

'One day I'll bring Pickles round to you, then the two of you can play all day.'

I can't help smiling. Perhaps this Barnie isn't such a bad type after all. I mean, my *mom* likes him.

My mom has another cup of tea and Barnie orders me a milk shake. He and my mom are laughing and chatting all the time while I open my lucky dip. Once he leans over and says something in my mom's ear. She looks shy, and she blushes. And suddenly I know, now she's happy.

Barnie goes out of the Waldorf with us, carrying my mom's parcels. On the Parade he buys my mom a huge bunch of red roses. My mom is terribly glad, but she doesn't want to show it, so she tells him, 'No Barnie, you shouldn't . . .' But he pushes the roses into her arms, hooks his arm through hers and leads her to his Hudson which is parked nearby. He takes us back to Parow in the car. My mom and I have both forgotten about the lace she still meant to get at Spracklens.

My mom puts the roses in a glass vase and tosses an Aspro into the water. 'That keeps them fresh much longer,' she says. The vase used to be my grandma's, and my mom has never used it before, it always stands in the showcase in the sitting room.

'Better not say anything about the flowers to your dad, Gertie. You know how he is. He doesn't like other people paying any attention to me.'

She puts the roses on the kitchen table. 'Here I can look at them every day, you see. They're so lovely. We really must plant a few rose trees of our own, but your dad doesn't like doing things in the garden.' She sits down at the table, lights a Cavalla and gazes at the roses for a very long time without saying a word.

After a while she looks at the alarm clock on the dresser and starts. 'Goodness me! Look at the time. Your dad will be here any minute. Tonight it's just going to be fish and chips, sorry to say. Gertie, go and rinse the coffee bag under the tap.'

Soon after New Year, my dad says, he and old Cottage Pie will have to go back to Touws River. There's big trouble over there. A lot of stuff has been stolen.

'It's going to cost the Railways hundreds of pounds. They've fiddled with the books too. Seems to me they'll have to call in the Railway police.'

'But what about the guards? Are they asleep on duty?' asks my mom.

'They're in it together,' says my dad. 'And the ones that aren't stealing can't keep up with all the schemes the others think up to carry things through the gates. You know, there was this shunter, every single day of his life, ever since he started working there, he carried one brick home in his sandwich box, and by the time he went on pension he had enough bricks to build himself a brand-new house.'

'Go on!'

'I'm telling you. You'll be amazed. Another bloke took home a piece of copper every day, and you know how expensive copper is, hey? And d'you know how *he* got past the guards?'

'Yes?'

'Everybody knew this bloke was fond of plants and every time they saw him he was carrying a pot plant or something. Well, in the bottom of that pot, under the soil, he was hiding the copper. And so he got past them for years.'

'And now you got to go back to Touws River? I must say, you seem quite happy about it.'

'No, Doris. A man gets tired of living in the barracks. Every night it's the same food and everything, but I happen to be a stock verifier and my job is my job. It's no use complaining. After all, I'm doing it for *you*.'

'So I suppose I'll just have to ask Mrs Kok Bok for a favour again to take Gertie in at night.'

'You know, Doris, I think I'm earning enough by now to look after you and Gertie. We got all we need. Why don't you give up the bio-scope now? Your place is here at home. That's where a woman belongs. It's not as if we need the money.'

'Piet, are you starting all over again?'

'Ag Doris, it's no life for a man, you know. To come home at night and find your wife out on the streets until God knows what time.' My dad's really pleading with my mom now.

He's a different man since he's come home from Touws River and much more friendly with me. Once when he got back pay he even bought my mom a pair of pink slippers with high heels and pom-poms, and for me a gold signet ring with a heart, and my name written on it. My mom says it's eighteen carat gold.

Now it looks as if my mom is going to give in to my dad again. She blows the ash from the tablecloth and says, 'We'll see about that, Piet, we'll see, but not right away. First Mr Reid will have to find another girl in my place. It's not easy to find a good usherette and only last month they had to sack two girls.'

My mom takes me to the Jacobs kids to play with them all morning. She helps me dress, and she says, 'You shouldn't spend all your time with the grown-ups like this. You need friends your own age. Come on, put your arm into the sleeve.'

'Dad said I'm not allowed to play with the Jacobses.'

'Well *I'm* telling you to go and play there, so stop being stroppy. I'll tell your dad when he comes back from Touws River.'

'I don't want to, Mom. I want to stay here with you.' I begin to cry.

'Well, only for today then. I've got business to do. I'll come and pick you up just now.'

'I'm not going!' I scream.

I can see my mom's getting angry. She stamps her foot on the floor. 'Now cut the crap and stop talking to me like that!'

It gives me such a fright I stop crying right away.

'If I tell you to do something you *do* it, okay? Now do you hear me?'

'When are you coming to pick me up?'

'As soon as I've finished my business.'

'What are you going to do then?'

'None of your business.'

I start crying again, softly. My mom has never spoken to me like this before.

'Now come on, be a good girl,' she says. 'You really shouldn't be among grown-ups all the time. Come here, let me wipe your mouth. And then go and see if there's any eggs before we leave.'

My dad says the Jacobses are Sappe and all they know something about is the royal family. Their whole stoep is covered with Union Jacks and above the wireless in the passage is a portrait of Princess Margaret and Princess Elizabeth.

Mr and Mrs Jacobs have ten children. The oldest ones, Lily and Doreen, are married already. Lily's husband is in jail and she lives in the back yard with her two kids named after the English princesses, Margaret and Elizabeth. Lily has no front teeth and she's always shouting at the kids. 'Just like a bladdie coloured meid,' says my dad.

Old Mr Jacobs is nicknamed Jan van Riebeeck. He always wears a wide-brimmed hat and an old-fashioned suit with a waistcoat and a Zobo with its chain showing. He's got a long beard and a red face, and my dad says it's from drinking. He and his sons, Tom and Brian, are always tippling, says my dad. Every evening they sit in the bar of the Central Hotel until they close the doors. Then they come home and beat up everybody. That's why that brood of children are so dumb. The whole lot of them are in the special class at Parow Primary. All you can teach those kids is knitting and woodwork. My dad says they're a bad lot and they're half-bloods. You can see it in Grace, one of the daughters, in her frizzy hair. And then she's so stupid even her teeth are falling out. All she can do is make soup and that's probably made of dishwater and sweet potatoes. 'A lot of kwaggas, those Jacobses . . .' says my dad.

'I mean, just take that Grace with her frizzy hair and her thick lips. She couldn't even pass standard two. So old Jacobs took her out of school to work at home. Now it's time for her to get confirmed in the church, but old Minnaar, the elder, tells me she can't even recite the Lord's Prayer, let alone the Ten Commandments.'

There's a party at the Jacobs place every Saturday night, says my dad. 'Every skollie in Parow drops in and they dance all the way down the passage, out on the stoep, into the kitchen, and then all the way back again, through the passage to the stoep. Right in front of the children. And those kids just lie about on the stoep and when nobody's looking, then one of them, that boy with the freckles and the scabby heels, starts smoking one cigarette after the other. I won't be a bit surprised if he takes a swig on the sly too.'

'Piet, how do you know all this?' asks my mom. 'You peeped through the hole in the fence at the back again. One day they'll be catching you, just you wait.'

'Well, I don't want to see Gertie mixing with that lot. They're not our class and those kids are much too forward. Gertie'll see things not meant for her eyes. You know what they say about getting wise before your time, hey . . .?'

'Forget about the Jacobses, man. Why do you always keep on and on about a thing like that?'

'Yes, but one's got to . . .'

'I know: improve yourself.'

'Hell, but you're grumpy tonight, Doris, what's the matter with you?'

'I'm not grumpy, and why can't you talk about something else for a change?'

'What'd you like to hear?'

My dad gets up with the fly-swat and swats at something on the wall. 'I'm just saying. I don't want to see Gertie mixing with them.'

I've been playing hopscotch and hide-and-seek with Miena and Dolfie Jacobs all morning and when I get tired I go to sit with Mrs Jacobs on an old car seat on her stoep. Right next to her is a tyre, cut open and painted silver, hanging from a length of rope. Plants with all kinds of colours are growing in this tyre. Mrs Jacobs says they're Joseph's Coats, and the more the leaves catch the sun the more colours they show. There's also a rusted golden syrup tin with a lot of hen-and-chickens in it.

Mrs Jacobs is paralysed in her lower legs and all day long she crochets baby booties and doilies which Lily sells in front of Swanepoel's butchery in Main Road on Saturday mornings.

Mrs Jacobs says the doctors can't do anything for her. She's been to a whole lot of them. They can't find out what's the matter with her at all. She just woke up like that one morning. When she tried to get up, she was paralysed. Her legs wouldn't move. All the life had gone out of them so now she spends her days on the stoep. But now she's heard about a man from America who's come here with an aeroplane to heal people with prayer.

'The blind can see and the deaf hear. The lame and the maimed throw away their crutches and start walking. That man performs miracles. But your faith's got to be strong,' says Mrs Jacobs. 'If you don't believe, it's useless.

'Perhaps I can get to that man – I've forgotten his name now, it's English, like Bran-something – if only somebody can take me out to Wingfield. Is your dad's car still broken? That's where he's got his tent.

'They say this Bran-man has healed hundreds of people with his prayers. The people come from all over. In ambulances, on the backs of trucks, even on stretchers. They say sometimes there's so many sick people they've got to go home and come back again in the morning. Some of them even spend the night there in the open. Right there in the veld.' She sighs. 'If only my old man had a car . . .'

I'm fast asleep when my mom comes to fetch me. 'My poor child,' she says, and then to Mrs Jacobs, 'Thanks, Mrs Jacobs. I owe you one for this, hey?'

There are new roses in my grandma's glass vase when we come in through the kitchen door. 'So that Barnie's been here again, has he, Mom?' I cry. 'Ag sis, man. And where's my monkey, and why can't I be here when he comes over? He *said* he'd bring Pickles with him. Was Pickles here?'

'Shh,' says my mom. 'I bought these roses myself. The others were so lovely that I bought myself a new bunch when I went to the market this morning.'

'Oh. But when's my monkey coming then?'

'Gertie, I told you these things take time. Uncle Barnie's got to look around for one. Monkeys are hard to come by, man. You've got to be patient. One can't expect everything to happen overnight.'

'Mavis, I've got to talk to you,' my mom says to Aunt Mavis in the kitchen one morning. 'It's about Gertie and this monkey you promised her.'

I'm sitting outside the kitchen door under the verandah, on the steps. My mom doesn't know I'm there, because when Aunt Mavis turned up she sent me to go and sit outside by the gate to see what's going on there. It's too hot out there, so that's why I came back here.

'What about the monkey?' Aunt Mavis pretends to be all dumb.

'You promised the kid she'd get a monkey. Remember? That was before the dance.'

'I thought she'd forget about it.'

'That'll be the day! That's what *you* think. The kid can't think about anything else, and you're the one who promised her a monkey. So what now, Mavis?'

Aunt Mavis doesn't answer.

'Have you asked Barnie? Told him to get Gertie a monkey on one of his trips like you promised?'

'But Doris, be fair, man. Where'll he get a monkey? That one he's got he brought back from up North. Years ago.'

'You promised the kid, you know? Shame on you, Mavis.'

'Anyway, Piet won't allow her to keep a monkey and you know it.'

'One shouldn't lie to a child, Mavis. She'll never trust you again, you know.'

'Now don't you start preaching to me, Doris.'

'What am I going to tell Gertie?'

'Think up something. Tell her the monkey died on the goods train on his way here.'

'I won't lie to my child.'

'Well, okay then, Doris, give me a chance to think of something. Perhaps I can put an ad in the *Argus*.'

'You'd better come up with something, Mavis, because that kid's been waiting for her monkey for weeks now. You can't do this to her. She's put her heart on it. She even wanted to buy him a Christmas box.'

'Shame, Doris, I never thought she'd take it to heart like that.'

'Well, you don't know kids.'

'I've also got a kid . . .!'

'Yes, but that's different, I mean Caroline . . .'

'What do you know about Caroline? What do you know about what's going on inside her?' Aunt Mavis bursts into tears.

'I didn't mean it like that, Mavis. Don't get me wrong, man.'

'Well then, don't tell me I don't know a child's heart.'

'Ag, Mavis.'

'How d'you think a mother feels when they put her child in an institution?'

'Have a drink, Mavis. I'm terribly sorry, man, I really didn't mean to hurt you. All I wanted to say was that Gertie's heartbroken about the monkey and you can't drop her now.'

'God is my witness, Doris, I'll walk my shoes to the uppers to find a monkey. For Gertie. I have a child of my own and even if it's different today, I'm a mother at heart. No-one can ever accuse me of not caring about a child.'

'Okay, Mavis, I know. It's the honest truth you're talking and I know that. It's just been a misunderstanding. I know you, you've got a heart of gold. Gertie can wait a while longer. Maybe I'll talk to Barnie myself tomorrow. Perhaps he knows something about a monkey or whatever.'

I've heard every word they've been saying. So, Aunt Mavis has lied to me about the monkey. And so, that's what's going on here at home when my mom takes me to the Jacobses to play with the kids. It's that Barnie man who comes over to see her. So why can't I be at home when he comes? What do they talk about? What are they saying that I'm not supposed to hear? I'm going to tell my dad everything.

'Have another drink,' says my mom.

'I see you're also drinking White Muscadel now?'

'Ag, it's just a bit that's left over from a bottle Barnie brought round the other day.'

Aunt Mavis laughs. 'And what'll Mister Van Greunen say if he finds out there's another man calling on his wife in the daytime?'

'It's not what you think, Mavis. It's all innocent. We're just good friends, that's all. After all, Gertie's here too. Barnie's so lonesome and I feel sorry for him. Can't one be friends with a man?'

'Sackie George!' cries Aunt Mavis.

'Ag bugger you, Mavis!'

'See no evil, hear no evil, speak no evil . . .'

I kick open the kitchen door and yell at them, 'I'm going to be sick!'

My mom comes running to me and takes me to the bathroom.

I throw up all my food. With the back of her hand my mom checks my forehead. 'You've got a fever,' she says and takes me to the bedroom.

Aunt Mavis comes after us, looking at my mom in a half-scared kind of way. 'Little Blue-eyes!' she says, 'What's the matter then?'

My mom draws the curtains and I give Aunt Mavis a really dirty look, even worse than my dad gives the Jacobs kids.

That evening I refuse to go and sleep at Mrs Kok's. I just carry on crying and crying and crying. My mom brings me custard and jelly, but I throw that up too.

'What's the matter, little Gertie?' asks my mom.

'I don't want you to go and work tonight, Mom. Please stay with me.'

'It's all right, my darling. Mom'll stay with you all night, you can sleep in the double bed with me.'

'And I'm not going to the Jacobses tomorrow either,' I cry.

'Ag shame, man. Has Mom been neglecting her little baby? No, of course you needn't go. You can stay right here with me, I'll make you something nice to eat.' She gets up. 'I'm just going to write Mr Reid a note to tell him I'm not coming tonight. I'm going to ask old Boeta van der Merwe to give it to him, okay?'

'That Barnie man's coming today, isn't he?' I say to my mom the next morning.

'Where on earth did you hear that?' asks my mom.

'I heard you telling Aunt Mavis yesterday.'

My mom keeps standing at the sink for a long time, her hands in the dishwater. Then she wipes her hands on her apron and comes to sit with me at the table where I'm busy with my colouring book and my crayons.

'Gertie, I want you to listen very carefully to me today. Look at me. Put down those crayons.'

I look at my mom. Her eyes are a real see-through blue. I've never seen her looking quite so beautiful before. I feel like leaning against her so she can hold me tight. I don't want anybody else to be near us, not even my dad. As far as I'm concerned he can stay in that bladdie Touws River for ever.

My mom takes my hand and I feel like crying. She gets more and more beautiful as she sits there opposite me on her chair in her half-naked dress and with her see-through eyes.

'Look, it's true that Uncle Barnie sometimes comes over to our place,' says my mom. 'And it's true that he sometimes comes here when you're over at the Jacobses. But it's not because I don't want you here. No, Gertie,' says my mom, shaking her head. Her long blonde hair is bobbing beside her head, almost up to her mouth. I can barely hear what she's saying. She keeps on talking and talking, saying that sometimes grown-ups feel like having a chat among themselves without any kids around.

'And it's not good for the kids either. A kid's got to learn to be happy playing with her own friends.'

I get off the chair and go over to her, putting my head in her lap. I can smell my mom, and without meaning to I start crying again.

My mom strokes my hair. 'What's the matter with you, my little baby girl?'

'I feel sick.'

Once again I throw up all my food and my mom takes me to her bed and comes to sit beside me.

'Will it be better for you if I stop working and stay home with you and your dad?'

'Ye-e-es,' I sob. 'And I don't want the monkey any more either.'

My mom licks off the knife. She's busy icing the cake she's baked for my grandpa.

'Here's a hollow in the cake. You weren't keeping still in front of that oven door. The air got in. Now I'll have to fill it up with icing.'

'The Williamses at the back are moving. They've packed everything on the lorry.'

My mom looks up. 'Where on earth will they be going to? Have they got any place to stay? Has Gregory said something?'

I shake my head.

'I have a good mind to give *them* the cake. They're a damn sight better than the lot around here.' My mom points with the knife.

She sits down at the kitchen table, her chin on her hand. 'Yes, I'm going to give them the cake!' she says, and she gets up, takes out a plate and puts the cake on it. 'We can buy your grandpa something else from the Homepride when he comes tomorrow.'

I follow my mom, through the front gate and round the corner to the Williamses'. They're just getting ready to drive off. The man is moving in behind the wheel and Gregory and his mother are already seated.

My mom goes round to Gregory's mother's side with the cake. 'I just came over with a little something to celebrate your new place,' she says, holding out the plate with the cake on it to the woman.

Gregory's mother looks at her and says, 'We don't need anything, thank you, Madam.' Then she turns her head and stares out through her window.

The man just remains sitting behind the wheel without moving.

His wife says to him, 'For God's sake, get a move on so we can get out of this place!'

He turns on the engine and starts reversing the lorry.

My mom runs after them, still holding the cake, and shouting: 'We're not all like that!' But the woman winds up the window in her face. They drive off without once looking back at us, Gregory and his mother and father.

I look at my mom and I can see she's crying. I put my hand in hers and we go back home with the cake.

My mom puts the cake on the dresser. 'Well, they can go to hell then!'

My dad sends word from Touws River to tell us he'll have to stay on for another week or two. It's a big job they've got on their hands. The Railway police have been called in and it seems as if the high bucks in Touws River, the mayor and the magistrate, are also involved in the stealing. There's talk about five thousand pounds' worth of stuff that's missing.

If the matter goes to court my dad may also have to be called as a witness. The newspapers will get wind of it and start reporting about it, most likely.

But he himself is well, my dad writes. The dry air seems to be doing his chest a power of good and the asthma is clearing up.

'Dash it all!' says my mom, very annoyed, throwing the letter down on the kitchen table. 'What a way to start the new year, with your father away from home more often than not.

'It means you'll have to sleep over for a few more nights at Mrs Kok's. But it won't be for long. I can't promise anything yet, but I'm thinking of giving notice to Mr Reid. Then I can be at home all the time.'

Uncle Tank and Aunt Mavis don't come over as regularly as before. Just after Christmas Isaac Levitt's lorry drivers skedaddled, so he called in Uncle Tank.

He's working himself to death, moans Aunt Mavis. 'He leaves before dawn and only comes home after dark. Still, I'm happy for him, Doris. It makes him feel needed.'

Aunt Mavis has become friendly with a new usherette, a Lydia Somebody, who's also started at the Victoria bioscope, and now she'd rather visit there than here. My mom says as a matter of fact she's glad about it, because the two of them used to keep her from her work. Now she's got time for other things. And perhaps Uncle Tank will at long last find his feet again. Maybe Aunt Mavis will appreciate him more if he's no longer around all day to fetch and carry for her.

'Who knows, perhaps Isaac Levitt will give Uncle Tank a steady job, even if it's really only a job for coloureds.'

My mom still takes me to the Jacobses from time to time to spend the morning with the kids, because she says I'll be a big girl soon and I've got to learn to mix with other kids. She doesn't want me to fall behind, it can hurt me for life.

'As soon's your dad is back from Touws River we can go out a bit more over weekends,' she promises. 'I can prepare us a basket in the evening, then we can drive out to Campers Paradise in the Plymouth on the Sunday. Otherwise we can go to the docks for the afternoon to watch the ships and maybe buy us a few nice crayfish.'

Sometimes, my mom says, there are ships from other countries in the docks and then one can go up with the ladder and walk about on the ship to have a look around. It's just like a city of its own, says my mom, only a bit smaller, with shops and cafés and ballrooms and bioscopes and hairdressers and everything. There are even places for kids to play, with seesaws and swings.

One can talk to the sailors too, except when they're from Russia or Japan. They're not allowed to talk to the people of the countries they visit. They're the enemy.

Many of the sailors bring hundreds and hundreds of boxes of matches from their homes in their own countries and then they exchange it for our matches. Lots of people collect matches from all countries of the world as a hobby.

She'll talk to my dad, my mom says, then he can take us so I can see what a ship looks like inside. It's really something very special.

'And,' promises my mom, 'when the merry-go-round comes back I'll take you so you can ride on the horses.'

We can drive to the sea too, one afternoon, says my mom. She sighs. 'The days are so beautiful. And the Plymouth is just gathering rust in the yard. We can go to pick up shells. Blouberg is the best place for shells. Some of them look like real little stars and others like tiny, tiny green pumpkins. There's bigger shells too, like the one on the sideboard. If you hold the open end to your ear you can hear the sea.'

We can do all these things over weekends, as soon's my dad comes back. But in the week I have to go to the Jacobses one or two mornings to play with the kids so that she can have time for doing her own things.

I nod. My mom has such a nice way of talking and I know she'll talk to my dad about the weekends when he's back. She never sommer says something, she keeps her word. She's not like that.

'So why don't you keep Mrs Kok company for a few more nights too? She's so lonesome with old Kok Bok working night shift.'

We play all morning under the bluegum trees near the run of the Muscovy ducks. We've put on the grown-up clothes Lily has given us. We've also put on lipstick and make-up.

When we get tired of playing housey, Dolfie wants us to play weddings. He'll be the husband and me his wife. Miena can be the dominee who marries us.

I put on one of Lily's long dresses over my own and Miena winds a length of old lace curtain round my head.

After the wedding we drink water from Miena's tea set, pretending it's wine. Then Dolfie says he and I must go to bed now, because as soon's one is married you go to bed. From now on we'll be sleeping in the same bed, because I'm his wife now. When you're married, husband and wife sleep in the same bed.

Miena starts to laugh. 'You got to take off your clothes too, otherwise you're not really married.'

'No,' I say, because I don't feel like getting into bed with Dolfie at all.

'You got to,' says Dolfie, taking me by the arm.

'If a man and a woman go to bed together without being married it's a helluva sin,' says Miena, laughing again. 'They do all kinds of bad things.'

'Before the husband and his wife go to bed they take off all their clothes and then they look at each other,' says Dolfie. 'They also feel each other.'

'Now you must take off your clothes, Gertie,' says Miena and she pulls the lace curtain from my head.

'You must take your panties off too,' says Dolfie.

I get scared and begin to cry.

'Crybaby!' they yell, pulling at my long skirt. It falls over my feet and I kick it off and cry worse than before.

'I'm going to tell my mom.'

'Well, bugger off then!' shouts Miena.

Leaving my doll behind in the dust I run out of the gate, round the corner, back to our house.

I open the kitchen door. The house is dark and silent. I want to call out to my mom, but something doesn't feel right. I'm getting hot. My heart is throbbing very hard and loud and I'm beginning to feel a bit sick. I tiptoe to the sitting room, but my mom isn't there. So I go to her and dad's bedroom. The door is closed. Very softly I turn the knob.

It's half dark in the bedroom. My mom and Barnie's clothes lie strewn all over the chair in the corner.

They're on the bed and they don't have any clothes on. Barnie is lying on top of her and her legs are drawn up over his white hips. They are jerking and somehow they seem to be stuck together.

My mom is lying with her head thrown back on the pillows. Her long blonde hair is all in a mess and damp on the sides of her head.

'Oh,' she cries, 'oh . . .!'

Then she lifts her head and presses her mouth against Barnie's neck and starts speaking with her teeth against his skin. I can't make out what she's saying. Her arms are round his body, under his arms, and I can see her scratching him with her long red nails until it bleeds.

Barnie half gets up on his knees and starts moaning like someone in pain. Over and over he says my mom's name.

'Doris, Doris . . .'

The way he says my mom's name makes me feel very lonely and sad. The room smells like warm moss.

I look at Barnie's bare body which is half inside my mom's, and I see them jerking faster and faster.

My mom's head falls back on her pillow once again. She pushes her hands under her head and starts turning her face this way and that while her lower half is moving on its own. Then she begins to scream.

Barnie stretches himself over my mom's body, lies down on her again and takes her in his arms. 'Darling,' he says. 'Darling . . .'

My mom is sobbing loudly now, covering her eyes with her hands. 'Oh it's wonderful!' she cries.

I turn round, close the door and run down the passage, through the kitchen, through the back door, all the way to the chicken run. I know nobody will hear me.

The sun is dazzling in my eyes. Down by the wire fence where Gregory and I always used to chat I sit down. The chickens come up to the fence, staring at me with their little eyes.

A childless old couple have moved into the house where Gregory once lived with his father and mother.

I begin to cry, because I don't want to go and spend the night at Mrs Kok Bok's again, and because I don't want to play with the Jacobs kids any more, and because Gregory has left, and because I miss my dad.

Two policemen came to tell us that my dad was dead. They said the doctor thought he had an asthma attack, and then he kind of choked, so his heart gave in. My mom was just preparing to go to the bioscope when they brought the news.

My mom gave notice at the Victoria bioscope just like that and I'd heard Uncle Tank tell Aunt Mavis that my mom didn't really need to work any more. The Railways looked after their people and we were well away, he said.

My grandpa and Aunt Mietjie came to spend a few days with us, until after the funeral. My mom bought black clothes and wore them every day. She had to mourn in black for a whole year, said Aunt Mietjie, adding that by rights I also had to wear black, but my mom wouldn't allow it. My mom didn't want me to go to the funeral either, because she said I was still too young to understand.

Most of the time I spent with Aunt Mavis and them. She said my mom had lots of things to fix up now that my dad was dead.

My mom was very quiet and kind of different. She hardly ever spoke to me and sometimes she didn't even seem to know I was there. She would look right at me, but it was as if she was looking at something else.

Aunt Mavis told Uncle Tank she thought it was a bad sign that my mom hadn't cried yet.

'It's not natural, Tank. Sooner or later this thing is going to catch up with her and then I really don't know.'

A few days later my mom found the asthma pump in the drawer of the chest on my dad's side of the bed. She sat down on the bed and started crying softly. 'It's all my fault that Piet died. The last time he left I didn't even pack his suitcase for him.'

She sat staring at the pump for a long time and her face changed. Slowly she picked up the pump, pushed the two tubes up her nose and pressed the ball.

'Scrrreech!' said the pump.

She coughed and pulled out the tubes. Then she pressed again.

'Scrrreech!' blared the pump.

Then my mom laughed – an ugly, loud laugh that went on and on.

I got scared and tried to snatch the pump away from her, but she pushed me aside and kept on pressing it, faster and faster.

'Scrrreech, scrrreech, scrrreech . . .'

I began to cry, but my mom didn't even hear me. The louder I cried the louder she laughed and the more noise she made with the pump.

I ran out the front door to Uncle Tank's rooms in Watering Street. I wasn't even scared of the dark. Aunt Mavis had already left for the bioscope and Uncle Tank was heating some food on the Primus.

He made me drink a few mouthfuls of sugar water and then took me by the hand and brought me home.

My mom was lying on her bed, shoes and all. She wasn't laughing any more, just staring in front of her. At first she didn't even seem to notice us. The pump was lying on the bed beside her. There were tears running down her cheeks.

Uncle Tank sat down on the bed next to my mom and took her hands. 'It's all right, girl. It's all right.'

My mom's shoulders began to jerk.

'It's natural, girl, have a good cry.' He picked up the pump and put it in his coat pocket.

'I'm taking this along with me. It's not good for you to be on your own like this. I'm going to get hold of that sister of yours.'

PART FOUR

EVER SINCE MY GRANDPA ALSO DIED, only two weeks after my dad's funeral, I slept with my mom on the double bed, on my dad's side. Sometimes I woke up in the night and then she held me very tight.

My mom was better now. She was much quieter and she'd stopped laughing, but Aunt Mietjie said she'd be all right. I just had to be patient, she said.

'These things take time. It's sorrow that's changed your mother. Just you listen to her when she talks to you, okay? She'll be her old self again. With your grandpa dead too it was a double blow, and that takes a lot out of a woman like your mother.'

Every day my mom sat in the kitchen with her legs crossed, a Cavalla between her fingers and a drink on the table in front of her. She'd sit there for a long time without saying a word.

After the first few days following my grandpa's funeral Uncle Tank and Aunt Mavis didn't come over much any more. When they did, they were always in a hurry somewhere else. The few times they did stay longer my mom hardly spoke to them and didn't even offer them a drink.

The Barnie man stayed away too. I think I heard Aunt Mavis telling my mom once that he was somewhere on a trip, but my mom hardly seemed to hear what she said.

One Saturday evening my mom went out to get an *Argus* on the corner at George's Café like in the old days and she took me with. We sat at the kitchen table afterwards and my mom told me bits of what she read while she was sipping her drink. It was almost the way it used to be.

Once she kept on reading something for a long time. She asked me to bring her the pencil from the dresser drawer and then marked something in the paper.

'Maybe this is the answer I've been waiting for,' she said after a while. 'I just have a feeling. Strange, I've had it all day.'

My mom poured another drink and finished it quickly. 'It's here in this advertisement.' She pointed at the piece she'd marked. 'Joe Harvey puts an end to all your problems. Experienced clairvoyant back from Europe.'

'Who's the man?' I asked. 'What's he do?'

'It's someone who can see into the future.'

I didn't understand and my mom explained. 'You see, a clairvoyant is someone with a special gift. It's a talent you're born with. You give them something you own, like this pencil, or a snapshot or a curler or something. Then they keep touching it until they go into a trance. The power of the thing you gave them gets hold of something deep inside you which you yourself don't even know about. They, the clairvoyants, catch this and then they know exactly what to do. In their mind they feel who and what you really are, what's still going to happen to you and what your chances for happiness are. Then they can give you the correct advice and tell you what to do with your life.'

My mom looked happy. I still couldn't understand properly, but I nodded and clapped my hands and laughed, because I was so happy that my mom was all right again.

She took the advertisement and went to dial the number in the passage. When she came back, she filled her glass again and held it up. 'Cheers! Here's to good luck! Joe Harvey's coming next Tuesday at ten o'clock.'

My mom emptied her glass where she stood at the sink, and then we went to bed.

Since my dad's death my mom hadn't gone to the bioscope again, not once. I rather missed the matinée once a month with her, from the time she still ushered. The Jacobs kids actually told me of a beautiful picture showing in the Victoria with Margaret O'Brien. I asked my mom whether we could go, but she just shook her head.

'One of these days, but not yet. One of these days I'll take you specially, Gertie, but right now there's other things I have to do first.'

One morning we heard a noise outside and my mom and I went out the front door to see what was happening. Everybody in the street was outside, crowding in front of Mrs Kok's house. There were two Black Marias too, and a big black car.

We went closer. A policeman stopped the people from going through the gate. He said they first had to look for fingerprints and footprints in the garden. They were investigating a case and everybody had to keep out and not even touch the gate.

'What's going on?' my mom asked Maizie Vlooi. 'Was there a burglary?'

'Doris, there's something terrible has happened right here in our street. When old Kok Bok came home this morning he found his wife dead in her bed, her eyes and mouth wide open and the bedclothes soaked in blood. Stabbed right in the heart with a knife.'

'No!' cried my mom, clapping her hand to her mouth. 'And Gertie's spent so many nights with her!'

'Yes,' Maizie Vlooi went on, 'they think it's that hotnot who always comes round on Tuesdays for bottles and bones. You know, the one who pretends to be soft in the head.'

My mom grabbed my hand. 'My child could have been killed with her!' she cried.

'Just shows you,' someone said.

Young Mrs Kleijn came to us. 'Poor old Kok's in a state. The doctor's been to give him an injection. Now he's lying over there in Mrs Haasbroek's sitting room on the settee. They still have to find out what's been stolen.'

'The bastard broke the window with a stone, right there by the handle,' she went on. 'Then he must've put his hand inside, opened the window and got in. With those deaf ears of hers she couldn't hear a thing, of course, the poor old woman.'

The crowd stood aside. Round the corner came an ambulance and stopped at the front door. Two men in white coats went into the house carrying a stretcher.

'Could have happened to any of us,' said Maizie Vlooi. 'Now you listen to me, I'm telling you it was that chap with the bottles and bones. Have you ever looked at his face? I just *know* it's him. I never trusted his face one moment. That's what I call a real murderer's face!'

'It's better not to trust a single one of them. Not even the good old sort. They're getting cheekier by the day. It's time the government did something about these bladdie hotnots.' Karel van der Merwe's mother had worked herself up into a proper state.

'How can one still sleep peacefully at night?' asked Maizie Vlooi. 'That's why I keep my Doberman pinschers. Those dogs can't stand the smell of the vermin and when they bite they bite to kill.'

'That's what *you* think,' said young Mrs Kleijn. 'They check out your house, poison your dogs and then they pounce. So what's the use?'

The people fell quiet again. The ambulance men were coming from the house carrying Mrs Kok on the stretcher, covered with a sheet.

My mom covered my eyes with her hands.

'Come, let's go, Gertie,' she said, pushing me all the way to our front door with her hands still on my eyes.

No, my mom told Aunt Mietjie and Uncle Koos one night when they were over at our place, Joe Harvey had made a fool of her. He wasn't a clairvoyant's backside. He came a few times, it cost her a packet of money, and she got bugger-all out of it – only humiliation!

'Like hell he's a clairvoyant! He's a randy old man, a real chancer, that's what he is! All that going into trances and turning up his eyes – a bladdie chancer! It gives me the creeps just to think of those blunt paws of his!

'And you know, Mietjie, Koos, in the beginning I quite believed him. But that was just because of his way of talking. No, he said, I must lie on the bed so he can hypnotise me and get in touch with my subconscious, because that's where the real problem lies. In my subconscious.

'Well, so I had to stare at a small shiny thing he held in his hand right in front of my eyes, trying not to think of anything. I had to try and imagine I'm seeing clouds. And that's where he started with his nonsense. I shudder to think what he'd have done to me if he'd really managed to put me to sleep.'

Uncle Koos burst out laughing. 'An old goat lusting after a green leaf.'

'All men are bladdie-well the same,' Aunt Mietjie said angrily. 'And where was Gertie while all this was going on?'

'She was on the pavement by the front gate.'

'So what did you do? I mean when Harvey started . . .?'

'No, I just jumped up. Right from the bed, shouting, "Ag no, sis man!" But actually I was crying, Jesus, Mietjie, can't you think? How would *you* feel? You put all your trust in someone who says he can help you, he can straighten out your life, you pay him a packet of money, and then he turns out like that!

'So, "Shame on you!" I told him. "You should be ashamed of yourself, doing a filthy thing like this to a poor unhappy woman whose husband only died the other day, and then you even take her money too! Now take your suitcase and get the hell out of here, or I'll call the police!"

'And you know what he said then? You know what he had the cheek to say? With a face as straight as anything he said he hadn't done a thing. That it was all in my mind. And why? he said, because I really *wanted* him to do something, and now I was accusing him because I felt ashamed about my own desires. He's going, he said, because he's a professional and he can't afford to get mixed up with women like me, it's bad for his reputation.

'Can you believe it, Mietjie?'

Uncle Koos started laughing again.

My mom and Aunt Mietjie looked angrily at him, as if to say, 'You just say something, Koos Brits! One word from you and you're going to get it!'

My mom was depressed now. 'It's hard to be a woman on one's own, with a child to bring up. And then to be made a fool of like this.'

The next morning my mom was very upset. She lay beside me in the bed, staring up at the ceiling and smoking one Cavalla after the other.

I tried to tickle her, but that just annoyed her and she said, 'Now don't you be a nuisance, Gertie, I'm trying to think.'

Later my mom got up, brought us coffee and got back into the bed. 'Your grandpa has appeared to me in a dream.'

'Has he got wings?'

'I didn't notice, I suppose he did.' My mom lit another Cavalla. She blew out the smoke, held the cigarette to one side and looked at it. 'He says he can see everything we're doing down here.'

It's really most upsetting, this dream she had about Pai, she later told Aunt Mietjie on the phone. 'There were tears in his eyes, you know, and he said he couldn't find rest, seeing us live like this. We got to repent, he said, and then his voice faded away. Then there was thunder and lightning and a voice said, "So sayeth the Lord thy God!" And suddenly it was all quiet again and Pai's voice came back. "Dorothea, Dorothea, Dorothea", over and over he said my name, over and over, but in such a sad voice. I'm so upset, Mietjie. D'you think there's something in it?'

One morning Maizie Vlooi came over and had tea with my mom at the kitchen table. When she left she said there was something she had to tell my mom.

'Doris, I think I'd better tell you. The other day there was a Slams over here at your place. He smeared stuff from a tin on your gate and on your front door knob. Must be pork fat. They use it to cast their spells. It attracts evil.'

'I don't believe in such things,' said my mom.

132

'Well, I just thought I'd better tell you, I mean well. And such things happen. It's all over the Bible.'

After Maizie Vlooi had left my mom poured herself a drink and said to me, 'Your dad was right. It's a bad lot in this neighbourhood.'

She didn't trust anything or anybody. Everybody lies to everybody else, she said, and there was something she hadn't told me about, but after that dream about my grandpa she'd gone to a spiritualist. A medium. A man near Green Arrow. A medium is someone who talks to the dead. He calls up the spirits of the dead to find out whether they're happy and whether there's something a person like her could do for them down here on earth so they can have peace.

She was taken into a room, said my mom, and they'd hardly settled down when the man started speaking to her to find out about my dad and my grandpa.

There was something ticking in the room, said my mom, like someone softly tapping with his fingers on a piece of wood. The man, he was called Burger, said there was something trying to get through. He could feel it. And then he went all weird, the whites of his eyes showed and he made a kind of rattling sound, his head drawn right back against the chair.

Then a voice came from the back of the room where there was a big cupboard. My mom said she had a terrible fright, but the voice said she was Mary and my dad wanted to give my mom a message through her. There was a curse on him, my dad said through this Mary-ghost. He could find no peace. And then the voice faded out. The Burger man came to his senses again and told my mom to come back on the Thursday night. Perhaps the Mary-ghost would have something more to say then.

My mom said this Mr Burger then started talking about the Jews. He said they wanted to kill off all the Christians and take over the world. They don't believe in Jesus and they're all communists. And they don't kill you outright, they cut off a vein in your neck and then they hang you upside down from a hook and let you bleed to death while you're scared out of your wits.

My mom said he then took out a book with pictures of animals hanging by their legs from hooks and bleeding to death and he told her that was what the Jews wanted to do to all of us. He belonged to an organisation, said my mom, that fought against the Jews and that was collecting money all over the world against the Jews. They already had a lot of money, but they needed much more. He said it was my mom's Christian duty to contribute.

My mom said the man went on talking and talking and she was listening very carefully, for she'd never heard anything like that before. And while he was still talking there suddenly was a hell of a crash. The very walls were trembling, said my mom.

'I looked round and saw a big fat woman lying on the floor, and the doors of the cupboard stood wide open.'

She had such a fright, said my mom, that at first she couldn't make out what had happened. And then she clicked. The fat woman had fallen from the cupboard. That was where she'd heard the voice of the Mary-ghost from.

'And there was no Mary any more,' said my mom, filling up her glass again. 'No, Mary was lying on the floor. What an idea to make such a fool of me! Mary had fallen asleep in the cupboard, of course.

'Well,' said my mom. 'That Burger man can go to hell and take his Jews and Maizie Vlooi with him for all I care!'

'Your mother is a seeker,' Aunt Mietjie told me one day when my mom was off to Bellville to see a woman who read palms. 'And I really have no idea of what she's seeking. All I know is your mother will never find peace for her soul. She just *can't* be satisfied with her life.'

My mom had always been like that, said Aunt Mietjie. Not like the other kids. She had a hell of an imagination. One day she'd believe she was a Spanish princess – *Spanish*, I ask you – who somehow ended up with my grandpa and grandma, and she told them that her true mother and father – that's the king and queen – would keep on looking for her so she could marry a prince who'd change her life. And other times she'd believe she was Anastasia.

'She even told me not to call her Dorie any more, the way we used to call her at home. She was Anastasia and that's how I had to call her. And if I wouldn't call her Anastasia, she said, she'd go and tell your grandma I'd stolen money from the collection in church.

'Your mother also wrote the weirdest essays at school. Heaven knows how she thought it all up. Your grandma once found her essay book and read what was in it. Good heavens, but the old lady was upset. And angry! She went straight to the school principal. She told him it was all wrong of the school to make kids write essays as it just taught them to lie.

135

'Well, and as she grew older it was the bioscope. I don't know why, but I suppose she found in the bioscope what she couldn't find in life. She could really *live* those stories, you know, like that time with *Gone with the Wind*.

'And now she's back at it. I suppose your dad's death has something to do with it, but once again she's running from one thing to the next and it's no use trying to talk to her.

'Just look at this business with the clairvoyant. One would think it would have taught her a lesson, but no – then she had to go to that medium in Green Arrow and look where she is today, at a palm reader, I ask you.

'And now your mother has told me she's going to that new De Vos church next week. They're holding services in the city hall in Cape Town. What on earth would she be going there for?

'I think it's because of those dreams she's been having about your grandpa. As soon's she closes her eyes, she says, your grandpa appears to her. I suppose she thinks if she goes to the De Vos church it'll soothe her conscience. Ag, I don't know. Perhaps your mother is just curious to see what's going on there. They split off from the Dutch Reformed Church, you see. All the papers are full of it. The churches are very much against the De Vos lot, they say they're just stirring up emotions. Every Sunday the dominees preach against them from the pulpit, they warn and rant and rave and beg and plead, but the people won't listen. They keep on streaming to the De Vos church and they say the city hall's chock-a-block night after night. I've heard that hundreds are converted every evening.

136

'Oh well, I suppose it can't do any harm. Your mother must do as she thinks best. She'll get over it.'

It was cold and I had to wear my red overcoat with the hood and my Fair Isle gloves. My mom was in a hurry. We had to leave early, because even though the city hall was a big place *everybody* was going and she wanted a good seat. It was a long time since she'd driven the Plymouth so the trip in to Cape Town was bound to take quite a while. My mom seemed to be looking forward to the occasion a lot.

There was a man in a black suit standing at the door of the city hall. He shook hands with everybody, saying, 'Welcome in the presence of the Lord.'

They called my mom 'sister' and gave her a book from which to sing.

All the people in the hall spoke to one another, even to us, although we didn't know them at all. They all seemed happy about something, but in an unusual kind of way. I don't know how to put it. Actually they were full of sights and it seemed as if everybody was trying to make up to everybody else. There were coloureds too, but they kept to one side of the hall. They didn't talk to us or look at us.

A man went on the stage and said we were going to sing now, sommer sitting down. He gave up a number and my mom looked up the hymn in the book. Then the man gave a sign and everybody started singing 'Now fill my lamp with oil' while he kept time with his hands.

The words of the whole hymn were just 'Now fill my lamp with oil' and we sang it over and over and over. It was an easy tune and after a while I could join in too.

After we'd been singing for some time the man on the stage held up his hands and stopped us.

'Brothers and Sisters, you're not singing like Christians. True Christians are joyful and happy, because they have reason to celebrate. Let's try again, and this time be *happy*!'

We started all over again. A few people began to clap their hands and soon the whole hall was clapping. This time it got very jolly and the man on the stage started bending his knees like he was doing the jitterbug, only he was staying in one place.

We went on singing for a long time before the preacher turned up. The man on the stage presented him as Brother Labuschagne.

Brother Labuschagne was a tall man with black hair and black eyes. He wore pointed shoes like Fred Astaire and while he was talking he kept on walking to and fro on the stage. Actually he was kind of sliding along, like he was stalking something. It was like a man doing the tango on his own, without a woman. His eyes were just as quick. When he looked at the people in the hall he seemed to see the lot of us in one sweep, looking each one in the face.

At times he spoke so softly that one could hardly hear what he was saying, and when he spoke softly like that it sounded as if he was crying.

He said, 'Have you heard Him knocking, Brother, Sister?'

Then he'd be silent for a long time before he asked the same question, over and over, louder every time, until in the end he was shouting at the top of his voice, '*Now* can you hear Him knocking?'

And then everybody started making a rumpus. Some shouted '*Yes, yes, yes!*' and '*Hallelujah!*' and all kinds of other things, words I'd never heard before.

My mom told me afterwards it was strange tongues. That happens when the Holy Ghost gets hold of you.

Then the preacher waited until the people were quiet again, and softly and sadly he said, 'Now He is standing at the gates of your heart. He is calling you! He *loves* you! Open up, open up, He pleads. Let me in!'

He took out a handkerchief, dried his eyes and said with a funny voice, half through his nose, 'You know, it is not so hard to give up sin, to say no to Satan. Give your heart to Him tonight and ask Him to lead you to the still waters your soul is yearning for so desperately, to peace and happiness, to Life Eternal, and He shall comfort you.

'But if you turn Him away from you tonight, Brothers, Sisters, then death and damnation await you, hell itself with its fire and brimstone, its suffering and anguish, world without end.'

I looked at my mom beside me. Her eyes were wide open and it seemed as if she'd had a hell of a fright.

After our fourth visit to the services of the De Vos church, when we got home, my mom unscrewed the lid of the White Muscadel bottle and poured all her drink down the drain, saying, 'Get thee hence, Satan!' She also took her box of Cavallas and threw it in the rubbish bin outside.

Ever since we started going to those services my mom turned all funny. I wished she'd become like she used to be before my dad died and all the other things happened to us. I was missing her, even at night while I was sleeping with her in the big bed. She was just thinking all the time, and when she was like that I knew I'd better leave her alone. So I just tried to remember what Aunt Mietjie had said, that she'd get over it.

In the evenings we drove in to Cape Town in the Plymouth and all the time my mom would hardly say a word to me. Only once she said it was time we had something done to the car, it was getting awfully rusty.

One evening we had a flat tyre in Maitland. My mom wasn't even annoyed. She just said, 'Oh well, it's the will of the Lord.' We got out and Mom signalled to the passing cars that there was something wrong with the Plymouth.

A coolie stopped and helped us change the wheel. My mom was so funny. She asked him if his soul was saved. The coolie just looked at her as if she wasn't all there.

When he left, my mom told him she'd pray for his soul. To me she said she'd known all along that someone would be sent to help us, because she'd been praying for help. It wasn't by accident that the Lord had sent a coolie to her. 'I can tell you, that coolie's got a lot to think about tonight.'

She wouldn't miss the last of the services for anything, said my mom, because the man was going to explain Revelations and those who'd been converted were going to give witness. We had to leave extra early. I had to take a nap in the afternoon because the service was going to last deep into the night.

So we left early, and just as well, because the city hall was already nearly full when we got there. The people were making more noise than before and they were even friendlier than before. They were all talking at the top of their voices. It was as if they were all expecting some terrible punishment, yet at the same time they seemed to be kind of happy about it.

I also felt a bit scared.

The preacher held up a pencil, a pair of pink high-heeled shoes and a packet of tea in the air. Then he asked two people from the front row to come on stage and read what was written on the stuff. He showed them where to look and both read out the same figures: 'Six six six . . .'

Everybody drew in their breath. One woman started crying and a man spoke up in a loud voice.

Then the preacher first took the pencil and threw it to the floor with all his might, followed by the pink shoes and the tea. The box broke and tea leaves were scattered right over the stage. Then the preacher kicked the stuff with his pointed shoe, sending it flying right through the door at the back of the stage. He was all angry and out of breath when he came to stand in front of the people again. His eyes were wide open and his hair hung right down over his forehead.

'This, beloved Brothers and Sisters, this is the sign of the Beast. The Antichrist. Six six six!'

The preacher seemed ready to topple over and he kept standing there like that for a long time, clutching his own body with his arms, before he could go on again.

'These are signs of the end coming and that day is nigh. It is oh so close. It is right upon us. We must heed the signs shown to us tonight.'

Now he's walking to and fro on the stage, speaking very softly at first and then louder and louder until it feels as if the words are beating down on us. You can actually see the whites of his eyes. There's going to be a war, he says, and a dragon with seven heads spitting fire. That's the communists trying to take over the world.

My mom puts her hand on her breast. She stares at the preacher, twitching her lips from time to time but not a word comes out of her mouth.

Once the preacher gets so tired he has to sit down on a chair for a rest before he can go on. Another man who is there to help the preacher gives us the number of a hymn to sing. It's an easy hymn, one only sings the words 'When Jesus comes on the clouds' over and over and over.

It is a sad sort of song and the longer it goes on the sadder the people get until some of them start to cry. I also feel like crying and I suddenly think of my dad who died because my mom had forgotten to pack his pump.

After the hymn the preacher speaks some more about the war and says we'll have to stand in a long line so the six six six can be branded on our foreheads and our wrists. These are the people who chose Satan rather than the merciful love of our Lord Jesus Christ. If we don't want them to brand us with the sign of the Beast our heads and hands will be chopped off and our blood will cover the earth.

Everything will be turned into blood, says the preacher. 'You will be thirsty and open the tap for water, but blood will come out of it.

'You will try to haul water from a well, but the water will turn into blood. An unquenchable thirst will overcome you and you will hasten to the fountains and the streams and the rivers, but all that water will be turned into blood. At last you will turn to the sea, but alas, one wave after the other washing ashore will be red, because the sea too will have turned into blood.'

I'm beginning to feel thirsty, but I don't want to bother my mom.

'A huge fire will come and consume all that lives and turn it into ashes. And when everything has been consumed so that there is nothing left, then Christ will descend. On the clouds He will descend to collect unto Him his children, those who haven't betrayed Him. And He will take them with Him to His kingdom in the third heaven, the paradise where the lion and the lamb shall graze together and where Life Eternal awaits them.'

The people in the hall are laughing and crying and talking together, all mixed up.

'Those who cling to the things of the earth, who visit the bioscopes and the gambling halls and the dancing halls, will suffer everlasting agony, because the fire into which they will be hurled will never stop burning.'

By now I really am terribly thirsty and my throat feels scorched.

Also, I'm getting awfully scared. What if the water in the tap has already turned into blood? I try my best to stop thinking about it, but I can't. I'm just getting thirstier and my ears are ringing.

'All those who have given their hearts to the Lord, put up your hands,' says the preacher.

Almost everybody in the hall raises their hands. Next to me my mom is saying a lot of funny words. I look at her and hardly recognise her. There are tears streaming from her eyes, running down her cheeks and dripping from her chin into her neck.

She puts up her hand.

When the preacher asks the converted to come to the stage, I put up my hand too. Perhaps they'll help me, I think, and give me some water, because it's no use asking my mom for it now. I don't want her to leave me behind on the seat either, while she lines up in front with all those other people. She's so weird, I'm afraid she may never come back.

So I go to the stage with her and it's only after some time that I notice I'm also crying loudly and my body is shaking. No-one notices or hears me and I know that if I speak to them they won't answer, they'll just go on crying and screaming and laughing. And what if the tap is filled with blood? But I'm *so* thirsty!

When we get to the stage I just can't stand it any longer. Stamping my foot, I start shouting at the top of my voice, 'I want water!'

The preacher looks at me and nods to a man to go and get me some water. The man comes back with a glass, but the glass is filled with blood.

'It's blood, blood, blood . . .!' I scream, and then I cannot stop my-self, I just run to the preacher and grab him by the arm, and bite his hand, and bite it, and *bite* it.

Some of the men try to pull me away, but I go on biting until I've bitten a chunk out of his hand. It tastes awful, kind of saltish, and yet not salty either. I spit it out and it falls on the floor, and then I stamp on it with my foot, shouting, 'Blood, blood, blood!' over and over.

The preacher turns to me and comes to me. 'This girl is possessed,' he says.

I feel so scared of the man I can't breathe or anything and there's white stuff coming from my mouth.

'She is possessed by the devil,' says the preacher, grabbing me by the shoulders and beginning to shake me very hard.

I still can't breathe, and I start choking on the stuff in my mouth. My head is throbbing and it feels as if my eyes are going to burst.

'In the name of our Lord Jesus Christ I command you to leave the body of this child!'

The preacher's black eyes are staring into mine and I cannot look away.

I suppose I must have fainted, because when I come to at last ev-erything is quite ordinary again. There's a lot of people crowding around me. The preacher is kneeling at my head.

'Look how calm she is now,' he says. 'The evil has left her.'

He is speaking in a gentle voice now and I'm no longer scared of him. I don't feel thirsty either. He picks me up in his arms and puts me on a chair. I feel very cold and my teeth are chattering. My clothes are all wet. They must have poured water over me.

The preacher puts his hands on my head. 'Bless her, Father, this precious pearl . . .' he says in his gentle voice.

Ever since my mom's conversion she hasn't had her hair cut or done any more. The upsweep has grown out and nowadays she fastens her hair with a bit of wool in her neck.

Sometimes she spends a whole morning at the kitchen table underlining words in the Bible with a pencil.

Aunt Mietjie says that's how it is with my mom and she'll get over it, but this time I'm not so sure. It is almost Christmas again.

No-one from the old days comes round to visit us any more.

Sometimes I sit in front of our gate on the pavement. I wait until the people in the street are close by, then I say, 'I was possessed by devils.'

They look at me in a funny kind of way, and then they laugh or go on. Then I shout after them, 'I'm converted now!'

'It's better, the way we live now,' says my mom. 'This is the way of truth. This is the happiness I've always been trying to find.'

If I want to go to the bioscope or somewhere else, my mom says those are worldly things, it belongs to the past. One day I'll understand it all.

She must be right, because all the people who come here with their Bibles and their books to read and pray for us, say so too. And that's what my grandpa also used to say. But sometimes I miss my mom the way she used to be with her drink and her Cavallas in the kitchen, with Uncle Tank and Aunt Mavis and the guitar; when my mom was still an usherette and made herself a beauty spot below one eye in the evening, and with the smell of Evening in Paris on her skin. I miss my mom with her long blonde hair brushing up against my mouth when she laughs like Spider Lady.

One morning my mom and I were going down the street. A car stopped beside us. It was Barnie in his open Hudson. Pickles was sitting on his shoulder. My mom turned round and looked at him.

'Hello, Doris,' he says, smiling with his gold tooth.

My mom didn't greet him. She just turned back, and took my hand and we walked on, her eyes straight in front of her.

Every Sunday and sometimes even during the week we go to a church service in a big tent on the stretch of open veld near the station.

Near the end of the service I always look up at my mom next to me. She gets prettier and prettier all the time, with those blue eyes that go all see-through-like. Her face shines, and I know it's the Holy Ghost that's got into her again. She opens her mouth and starts speaking those lovely words I have come to know by heart. The whole congregation falls silent, listening to the round, bright sounds coming from my mom's mouth:

'Halo Christu Ku Marrti Sen Bielef Tar Ty Salem Jawé Christu!! Rama Koerr Ja, O, Christu! Christu!!'

JEANNE GOOSEN is one of the most versatile writers in Afrikaans. She debuted as a poet in 1971 with her collection *'n Uil vlieg weg*, which was followed by *Orrelpunte*. She then made her mark as a playwright with a number of highly successful one-act plays and cabarets, such as *Kombuisblues*, *Kopstukke*, and *'n Koffer in die kas*. Some of her plays have been performed in Europe, in English and Dutch. But it is as a writer of prose that Goosen has carved a niche for herself in South African (specifically Afrikaans) literature. Her debut novel, *Om 'n mens na te boots*, was followed by *'n Kat in die sak, Louoond, Ons is nie almal so nie, o.a. Daantjie Dromer, Wie is Jan Hoender?, 'n Pawpaw vir my darling* as well as the short-story collection, *'n Gelyke kans*. *Ons is nie almal so nie* has been published in French and Dutch.

Goosen lives and works in Cape Town.